THE WONDERFUL ADVENTURES OF NILS

Selma Lagerlöf

Translated by Velma Swanston Howard
Revised by Nancy Johnson

SKANDISK
MINNEAPOLIS

....

THE WONDERFUL ADVENTURES OF NILS, BOOK ONE
First Skandisk, Inc. edition published 1991
Skandisk, Inc.
6667 West Old Shakopee Road, Suite 109
Bloomington, MN 55438

ISBN 0-9615394-3-7

Second printing, July 1993.

Third printing, June 1998.

Original English edition published 1907 by Grosset & Dunlap.
Translated from the original Swedish edition, published 1907 under the title
Nils Holgerssons underbara resa genom Sverige.

Cover and book design: Koechel Peterson & Associates, Minneapolis, Minnesota.

Manufactured in the United States of America.

....

Contents

A naughty boy who entered a magical world as Thumbietot (*tummetott*, in Swedish), a tiny imp, and learned the meaning of kindness and courage; a powerful tomten who had his revenge; a gaggle of wise wild geese; and an ornery fox all lived in Sweden a long time ago. They come to life again whenever a child reads *The Wonderful Adventures of Nils*. Commissioned by the Swedish National Teachers' Society as an introductory geography for schoolchildren, this is an adventure story, a folktale, a geography, and a history. It's a chain of short narratives, every one of them a masterpiece of the storyteller's art.

Author Selma Lagerlöf's fantasy has enchanted Sweden's children ever since it was first published in 1907 as *Nils Holgersson's underbara resa genom Sverige*. Translated into other languages, the story of Nils Holgersson's travels across Sweden on the back of a white gander is still popular. Germany's children have made it a best-seller. This 1991 edition, a revision of Velma Swanston Howard's translation from the Swedish, promises to become a cherished classic of English-speaking children the world over. As in the first English edition, some of the descriptive geographical detail in the Swedish original has been eliminated. The story itself is complete.

There was something very special about the author, Selma Lagerlöf. She was a novelist, a short story writer, an autobiographer, a poet, a biographer, and a dramatist. Herman Hesse, a recipient of the Nobel Prize in literature for 1946, said: "With her first work, *Gösta Berling*, she became famous in Sweden and very soon in the rest of the world. That first work was already perfect, containing all the essentials of the Lagerlöf gift...."

Synthesis of social comment, folklore and historical fact was characteristic of her work, and it is very evident in *The Wonderful Adventures of Nils*. Selma Lagerlöf's saga is as appealing now as when it was first created in the early 1900s. The problems addressed—poverty, sickness, draining of wetlands and deforestation, cruelty to animals, and child abuse, for example—are contemporary issues. Before she finished the book, Selma Lagerlöf wrote: "Through my reader, I want the young people to get an accurate picture of their country and to learn to love and understand it; I want them also to learn something about its many resources and the possibilities for development that it offers..." (letter to Josepha Ahnfeldt, November 18, 1904).

The author was born on November 20, 1858, in Mårbacka, Värmland, in southwestern Sweden. Her father was Erik Gustaf, a lieutenant in the Swedish army. Her mother's name, Louisa. Selma was the fourth of five children. The family was "lesser gentry," on friendly speaking terms with the nobility and receiving a certain nod of deference from the peasantry.

In 1863, when Selma was five years old, her grandmother passed away. That was a shock. Selma said: "My one recollection of her is of her sitting there day after day and telling stories from morning till evening.... It was as if the door to a wonderful magic world, in and out of which we had come and gone freely, had been locked...."

From 1881 until 1885 she attended the Stockholm Higher Teacher's College for Women, where she became fascinated with Scandinavian folklore. After her father died in 1885 and the family estate was sold, she supported herself by teaching at the Girls' High School in Landskrona. While there, she wrote her first novel, *Gösta Berling's saga* (*Gösta Berling's Saga*), which was published in 1891.

First the book was criticized for the mingling of fact with fiction. After it was given a favorable review by Danish critic Georg Brandes in 1893, *Gösta Berling's Saga* was reconsidered. Eventually it was applauded as not only Selma Lagerlöf's best novel, but one of the finest in Swedish literature.

Her first short story collection, *Osynliga länka* or *Invisible Links*, published in 1894, made it clear that her writing could be financially successful. She left teaching and became a professional writer. The door that had been locked when her grandmother died was open. Selma was a gifted storyteller, and the Swedish people loved her books. She even gained an international following, particularly for *The Wonderful Adventures of Nils*.

On November 23, 1907, this short paragraph about the book appeared in the *New York Times* under the title "Exciting Adventures for Boys":

"*The Wonderful Adventures of Nils* is the last and said to be the best book of Sweden's great fiction writer, Selma Lagerlöf, and the Swedish people say there has been nothing in their literature for children since Hans Christian Andersen to compare with it. It is the result of years of study of animal and bird life by the author, with legends and folklore, which are woven together into the charming story of little Nils, turned into an elf, traveling on the back of a goose with a flock of wild geese, understanding the speech of birds and animals. The book was brought out in Stockholm in December, 1906, and since then has been translated into German and Danish, in which it has been equally well received. It is translated into English by Velma Swanston Howard. There are delightful full-page and marginal pictures by Harold Heartt. (Doubleday, Page & Co.)"

Selma Lagerlöf was famous. In *The Wonderful Adventures of Nils*, she had created a remarkable tale of Sweden. That tale, with all of its insight and childlike delight, will be treasured for as long as there are children to read it.

In 1904 she received the Gold Medal of the Swedish Academy, and in 1914 she was elected the first woman member of that distinctive institution. In 1909 she was awarded the Nobel Prize in literature; she was the first woman ever to receive that honor. She used the money to buy back the entire Mårbacka estate, where she lived for the rest of her life. She died on March 16, 1940, at the age of eighty-one.

BIBLIOGRAPHY

Commire, Anne, ed. *Something About the Author*, Vol. XV, pp. 160-174. Detroit, Michigan: Gale Research Co., 1979.

Kepos, Paula, ed. *Twentieth-Century Literary Criticism*, Vol. XXXVI, pp. 228-249. Detroit, Michigan: Gale Research Inc., 1990.

"Exciting Adventures for Boys," *New York Times*, Vol. XII (November 23, 1907), p. 749.

THE TRAVELS OF
BOOK ONE
NILS HOLGERSSON

Chapter One

The Boy

The Tomten

Sunday, March twentieth.

Once upon a time there was a boy. He was about fourteen years old. He was tall and thin, and he had straw-blond hair. Nils was a good-looking boy; but, he was not a very good boy. Most of the time he only wanted to eat and sleep; and then if that bored him, he would get into mischief, sometimes quite serious mischief that got him into all sorts of trouble.

On this particular day, which happened to be a Sunday morning, his mother and father were getting ready to go to church. Nils sat by the kitchen table, thinking how lucky it was for him that they were going away. "Good!" he thought, "Now I can take Dad's gun from the gun rack and go hunting. Nobody will ever know."

Nils' father must have guessed what he was thinking, though; because just as he was about to go out the door, he stopped short and turned around. "Nils," he said sternly, "since you refuse to come to church with Mother and me, the least you can do is read the Lutheran service at home. Will you promise to do that?" "Uh…oh, yes, Dad," Nils responded. The boy intended, of course, to read only a little of the service.

Nils' mother (who knew him every bit as well as his father

did) went over to the shelf near the fireplace, took down *Luther's Commentary* and laid it on the table, in front of the window. Then she pulled up the big armchair on which, as a rule, only his father was allowed to sit. "Come here, Nils, and sit down," she said. "Oh, Mom," he thought, "what a waste of time—all this fuss and I'm only going to read one or two pages." Nils' father looked at him seriously, then warned him, "Now remember to read carefully, Nils. When we get back, I will ask you questions about the service; and if you have skipped one page, you will be sorry." "The service is fourteen and one-half pages long," Nils' mother added. "You will have to begin reading right now if you expect to finish before we return."

With a frustrated expression on their faces, Nil's parents left for church. As he watched them go, the boy thought, "There they go, congratulating themselves, I suppose. They think I'm so afraid of being punished that I will sit and study the sermon the whole time they are away." But his mother and father were not congratulating themselves; no, not at all.

There was a reason for their distress, and it was not that Nils might not read the service that morning. They were worried about his future. What would ever become of their rebellious boy? Life was difficult enough for hardworking people who cooperated with one another. Nils' parents were poor farmers, and their place was not much bigger than a large garden. When they first moved there, the place could not support more than one pig and a pair of chickens; but they were industrious and capable people, so now they were able to afford cows and geese as well. Things had turned out very well for them. They would have been satisfied and happy on that beautiful Sunday morning, if it were not for their son's disobedience.

Nils' father wondered how he could have raised such a lazy boy. Nils hadn't bothered to learn anything at school, and he never offered to help with the farm chores. He even complained about tending the geese. Nils' mother had to admit that all of this was true; but Nils could not get along with the neighbors either, and he was cruel to animals. "May God soften his hard heart and give him a better disposition," she said, "or else he will always be a problem to himself and to us."

Back at home, Nils wondered if he could get by without reading the Lutheran service. Balancing the fun of shooting his father's gun (which in itself might get him into trouble) against the switching he was sure to get if he did not read the service, he gave up any hope of disobeying his parents. This time he was trapped. Resigned to a dull morning, he plopped dejectedly into his father's easy chair and began to read. But after he had been rattling away in an undertone for a few minutes, he began to get sleepy—so very sleepy that he could hardly keep his eyes open, and his head began to nod.

Oh, and such a wonderful day it was! Cooped up inside the cottage, Nils could not enjoy the beautiful weather outside. Today was only March twentieth; but Nils lived in West Vemminghög Township, down in Southern Skåne, where the spring was already in full swing. The trees and fields were not yet green, but they were fresh and budding. There was water in all the ditches, and the colt's foot growing along the edges was in bloom. All the weeds that grew among the stones were brown and shiny. The beech woods in the distance seemed to grow thicker with every second. The skies were a bright, marine blue, and the air was deliciously warm.

The cottage door was open for fresh air; and although far off in the distance, the call of the lark seemed to fill the room. Hens and geese pattered about in the yard; and the cows, enjoying the spring air even in their stalls, lowed their approval.

Nils read and nodded and fought against drowsiness. "No! I will not fall asleep," he told himself fretfully, "because then I will never finish this service." But in spite of his struggle to stay awake, he fell sound asleep.

Nils did not know if he had slept only a short time or a long time, but he was awakened by a little sound behind him. The uneasy thought came to him that the door was open. Did someone enter the cottage while he was sleeping?

On the windowsill, facing the boy, stood a small mirror; and almost the whole cottage could be seen in it. As Nils raised his head, he happened to look in the mirror. The cover of his mother's keepsake chest was open!

Nils' mother owned a large, heavy, iron-bound oak chest, which she permitted no one but herself to open. Here she treasured all the things she had inherited from her mother, including two old-fashioned peasant dresses—of red, homemade cloth, with short, close-fitting bodices and pleated blouses—and a brooch decorated with pearls. There were starched, white linen caps, and heavy silver ornaments and chains. Swedish women no longer wore this style of dress, and several times his mother had thought of getting rid of the old things; but somehow, she could not part with them. They were too precious to her.

Nils could not understand why the chest drawer was open. He knew that his mother would never have left that precious chest open when he was at home, alone. All of a sudden, he felt goose bumps on his arms, and a chill went down his spine. Was there a thief in the cottage? Nils didn't dare to move. He just stared into the mirror.

What was that dark shadow falling over the edge of the chest? Nils stared at it. He did not want to believe his eyes, but the shadow grew until he realized that it was alive. A tomten was on the edge of the chest!

Now, Nils had heard stories about tomten; but he hadn't dreamed that he would ever see one. The creature was tiny, no bigger than a man's hand. He had an old, wrinkled and beardless face; and he was dressed in a black frock coat, knee-breeches and a broad-brimmed black hat. He was very neat and rather elegant-looking, with the white laces around his throat and wrists, his buckled shoes, and the bows on his garters. The tomten had picked up an embroidered piece, and sat and looked at the old-fashioned handiwork with such an air of respectful awe that he did not notice that Nils had awakened and was watching him.

Nils was surprised to see the tomten; but actually, he was not very frightened. It was impossible to be terrified of such a little creature. And since the tomten was so absorbed in his own thoughts that he neither saw nor heard, Nils decided to play a trick on him—to push him over into the chest and shut the lid.

But he was not courageous enough to touch the tomten with his hands; instead, he looked around the room for something to poke him. His gaze wandered from the sofa to the leaf-table; from the leaf-table to the fireplace. He looked at the kettles, then at the coffee urn, which stood on a shelf near the fireplace; on the water bucket near the door; and on the spoons and knives and forks and saucers and plates, which could be seen through the half-open cupboard door. He looked at his father's gun, which hung on the wall beside the portrait of the Danish royal family, and on the geraniums and fuchsias, which blossomed in the window. And last, he caught sight of an old butterfly net that hung on the window frame. He had hardly set eyes on that butterfly net before he reached over and snatched it. He jumped up and swung it at the tomten. Nils was astonished at the luck he had. He hardly knew how he had managed it, but he had caught the tomten. The poor little thing lay head downward in the bottom of the long net, and could not free himself.

At first, Nils did not have the least idea what to do with his prize. He swung the net backward and forward to prevent the tomten from getting a foothold and climbing up. Then the tomten begged—oh, so pitifully!—for his freedom. He had brought the Holgerssons good luck for many years, he said, and deserved better treatment. If Nils would set him free, he would give him an old coin, a silver spoon, and a gold penny, as big as the case on his father's silver watch.

Nils agreed at once. He didn't think the tomten had given him much of an offer; but it so happened, after he had the tomten in his power, that he was afraid of him. He felt that he had entered into an agreement with something weird, something that did not belong to his world, and he was only too glad to get rid of the horrid thing.

Nils held the snare still so that the tomten could crawl out. But when the tomten was almost out of the butterfly net, Nils had a greedy idea. "Maybe I could bargain for gold and all sorts of wonderful things. I could at least make the tomten conjure the Lutheran sermon into my head. What a fool I would be to let him go!" Nils began to shake the butterfly net violently so the tomten would tumble down again.

What a mistake! The instant that Nils shook the butterfly net, he received such a stinging blow on the ear that he thought his head would fall apart. He was knocked against one wall, then against another, until he sank to the floor, unconscious.

When Nils awoke, he was alone in the cottage. The chest lid was down, and the butterfly net hung in its usual place by the window. If he had not felt how his right cheek burned from that blow on the ear, he would have been tempted to believe the whole thing had been a dream. "At any rate, Dad and Mom will be sure to insist that it was nothing else," he thought. "They are not likely to make any allowances for that old sermon on account of my seeing a tomten. I had better try to finish that reading."

But as he walked toward the table, he noticed something remarkable. The cottage couldn't possibly have grown, but why did he have to take so many more steps than usual to get to the table? And what was the matter with the chair? It looked no bigger than it did before, but now he had to step on the rung first and then climb up in order to reach the seat. It was the same thing with the table. He could not look over the top without climbing to the arm of the chair.

"What in all the world is this?" wondered the boy. "The tomten must have bewitched the whole cottage!"

Luther's Commentary was on the table, right where he had

laid it down; but there was something strange about that, too, because he could not read a single word of it without standing on the opened book. He read a couple of lines, and then he glanced into the mirror on the wall. "There's another one!" He saw a little creature dressed in a hood and leather breeches.

Jumping up, he shouted, "Why, that one is dressed exactly like I am!" The tomten in the mirror jumped with him. With a horrible, sinking feeling, Nils began to pull his hair and pinch his arms and swing around; the creature in the mirror imitated every action perfectly.

Nils looked behind the mirror to see if a tomten was hiding behind it, but there was no one there. He began to shake with terror. He was thoroughly convinced that the tomten had bewitched him. The tiny creature whose image he saw in the mirror was himself.

The Wild Geese

Nils moaned, "I must be dreaming. If I wait a few minutes, I will become a human being again." Wishing as hard as he could, he stood in front of the mirror and closed his eyes. He opened them again after a few minutes. Nothing had changed; he was still the size of a tomten. Otherwise, he was the same as he had always been, with the thin, straw-colored hair, the freckles across his nose, the patches on his leather breeches and the darns on his stockings.

What was he going to do? It would do no good for him to stand still and wait; why, he might have to wait forever! He must try to find the tomten and win his forgiveness. Nils looked and looked; and while he looked, he cried and prayed and promised to change his attitude. He would never break his word to anyone again; he would never be mean; and never, never would he fall asleep over a sermon. If only he could be a normal teenager again, he would always be obedient to his parents. But all of Nils' crying and promises did not help him at all.

As he rubbed the tears from his eyes, he remembered that his mother had said the tiny folk made their homes in cowsheds.

Nils' face brightened, and he ran to look for his wooden shoes (he had been in his stocking feet ever since he got out of bed). Sure enough, there was a tiny pair of shoes on the doorstep. When he saw them, he was sure that the tomten intended that he be little for a long time. Nils pulled on his shoes and ran out the open door and onto the doorstep.

A gray sparrow hopping along the boardwalk in front of the cottage saw Nils and called out in surprise, "Teetee! Teetee! Look at Nils goosey-boy! Look at Thumbietot! Look at Nils Holgersson Thumbietot!" All the geese and chickens in the yard turned to stare at the boy, and then they started cackling. "Cock-el-i-coo," crowed the rooster. "Good enough for him! Cock-el-i-coo, he has pulled my comb." "Ka, ka, kada, serves him right!" cried the hens, and with that they kept up a continuous cackle. The geese gathered in a tight group, stuck their heads together and asked, "Who could have done this? Who could have done this?"

The strangest thing of all was that Nils could understand what they said. He was so astonished that he stood there as if rooted to the doorstep. "I must really be a tomten if I can understand what the birds say. Oh, how unbearable to hear those old hens say that it serves me right!" He threw a stone at them and shouted, "Shut up, you pack of silly chickens!"

It hadn't occurred to him that he was much tinier than they were. The whole yard-full of hens made a rush at him, formed a ring around him, and mocked him gleefully: "Ka, ka, kada, serves you right! Ka, ka, kada, serves you right!" Nils tried to get away, but the chickens ran after him and screamed until he thought he would lose his hearing. If the house cat hadn't come along just then, he might never have gotten away from the chickens. As soon as they saw the cat, they quieted down and left Nils alone, pretending to think of nothing else than scratching in the earth for worms.

"Dear Pussy," Nils said to the cat, "you must know all the corners and hiding places. Be a good little kitty and tell me where I can find the tomten." The cat did not reply at once. He seated himself, curled his tail into a graceful ring around his paws, and stared at the tiny boy. Pussy was a large, black cat with one white spot on his chest. His fur lay sleek and soft, and shone in the sunlight. The claws were drawn in, and the eyes were a dull gray with just a little narrow, dark streak down the center. Pussy seemed good-natured.

"Oh, I know where the tomten lives," he said in a soft voice, "but that does not mean that I will tell you where he lives."

"Dear Pussy, please tell me. Can't you see how he has bewitched me?"

The cat opened his eyes enough so that the green wickedness in them gleamed. He spun around and purred with satisfaction before he replied. "Should I tell you because you so often grabbed me by the tail?"

Nils lost his temper. He completely forgot how little and helpless he was, and ran at the cat. "Oh! Then I'll pull your tail again!"

That, too, was a mistake. How many mistakes can a boy make in one day! The cat was no longer a pussy, but a wildcat. Every separate hair on his body stood on end. His back bent; his legs stretched way out; his claws scraped the ground; his tail grew thick and short; his ears whipped back; his mouth frothed; and his eyes opened wide, glistening like sparks of red fire.

Brave because he did not know any better, Nils took another step toward the cat. The cat made one spring and landed on top of him, pinning him to the ground. His forepaws clamped down on Nils' chest, and his jaws opened wide over the boy's throat. Nils felt the cat's sharp claws sink through his vest and shirt and into his skin, and the sharp eye-teeth scraped over his throat. He screamed for help, but no one came to his aid. "I'm going to die!" he thought desperately.

"There!" the cat said, "that will do for now. I'll let you go this time, for my mistress' sake. Now you know which one of us is in power." The cat drew in his claws and let Nils go. Then he strolled off, looking every bit as friendly and innocent as when he first showed up. Nils was so crestfallen that he did not say a word, but only hurried to the cowshed to search for the tomten.

All told, there were only three cows in that shed. But when Nils entered the shed, they bellowed and kicked and made such a ruckus that one might easily have believed there were at least thirty cows. "Moo, moo, moo!" bellowed Mayrose. "There *is* such a thing as justice in this world." "Moo! Moo! Moo!" shouted the three of them in unison. Nils could not hear what they said because each cow tried to out-bellow the others.

Nils wanted to ask them where to find the tomten, but he could not make himself heard because the cows were in a frenzy. They carried on the way they used to do when he let a strange dog in on them. They kicked with their hind legs, shook their necks, stretched their heads and waved their horns menacingly.

"Come here, you!" said Mayrose, "and you will get a kick that you won't forget!" "Come here," said Gold Lily, "and you will dance on my horns!" "Come here, and you will taste how it felt when you threw your wooden shoes at me last summer!" bawled Star. "Come here, and you will be repaid for that wasp you let loose in my ear!" added Gold Lily.

Mayrose was the oldest and the wisest of the three cows, and she was the angriest. "Come here!" said she, "so I can pay you back for the many times you jerked the milk pail away from your mother, and for all the traps you laid to trip her when she came carrying the milk pails, and for all her tears when she stood here and wept over you!"

Nils wanted to tell them how he regretted all the mean things he had done to them and that he would never, never—from now on—do anything but good, if they would only tell him where the tomten was. But the cows made such a racket that they could not hear him. Fearing one of them would break loose and maul him, he left the cowshed.

Nils was thoroughly discouraged. He could see that no one wanted to help him find the tomten, and finding the tomten would probably do him very little good after all. Nils crawled up on the broad hedge which fenced in the farm, and which was overgrown with briers and lichen. There he sat down to think about what it would be like never to be a human being again. When his father and mother returned from church, there would be a surprise for them. The news of his being turned into one of the tiny folk would travel all over the land. People would come flocking from East Vemminghög, and from Torp, and from Skerup. The whole Vemminghög township would come to stare at him. Maybe his father and mother would show him at the marketplace in Kivik.

No, that was too horrible to think about. He would rather that no human being ever saw him again. No one could ever have been as unhappy as Nils was. He was no longer a human being, but a freak.

He was separated from everything and everyone now. He could no longer play with other boys, he could not take charge of the farm after his parents were gone, and certainly no girl would ever think of marrying him.

He sat and looked at his home. It was a little log house, which lay as if it had been crushed down to earth under the high, sloping roof. The outhouses were also small, and the patches of ground were so narrow that a horse could barely turn around on them. But little and poor though the place was, it was much too good for him now. He couldn't ask for anything better than a hole under the stable floor.

Oh, such troubles on a beautiful day! The weather was glorious, and Nils had never seen the sky as blue as it was today. Birds of passage were arriving. They came from foreign lands and had traveled over the East Sea by way of Smygahuk, and were now on their way north. They were of many different kinds; but he was only familiar with the wild geese, which came flying in two long rows that met at an angle, like the letter "V."

Several flocks of wild geese had already gone by. They flew high, but he could still hear their call, "To the hills! Now we're

off to the hills!"

When the wild geese saw the tame geese, they sank nearer the earth and invited, "Come along! Come along! We're off to the hills!"

The tame geese in the farmyard could not resist the temptation to raise their heads and listen, but they answered the wild ones very sensibly: "We're pretty well off where we are. We're pretty well off where we are."

This was an uncommonly fine day, an unusually fine day, one of those days that would linger in one's memory for a long time. The atmosphere must have been a real delight to fly in, so light and bracing. And with each new flock of wild geese that flew by, the tame geese became more and more unruly. A couple of times they flapped their wings as if they had a mind to fly along, but then an old mother goose would say, "Now don't be silly. Those poor creatures will have to suffer hunger and cold."

A big, white gander gazed in wonderment at the majestic wild geese flying so high and free. For the first time in his young life, he felt a passion for adventure. "If another flock comes this way, I'll follow them," he said to the tame geese around him. And when a new flock came overhead, calling, "Come along! Come along!" he answered, "Wait a minute! Wait a minute! I'm coming." He spread his wings and raised himself into the air, but he was so unaccustomed to flying that he fell to the ground again. "Wait! Wait!" he cried and made another attempt to fly.

Watching from the hedge, Nils thought, "It would be a big loss to Mom and Dad if the goosey-gander flew away. Maybe I can stop him." Once again he forgot that he was little and helpless. Leaping right down among the flock of geese, he threw his arms around the neck of the goosey-gander and hung on tight. "Oh, no! You won't fly away from here. I won't let you!" Nils cried.

But the gander was already in the air. He could not stop to shake Nils off, so the boy had to go with him.

Higher and higher they went, so rapidly that Nils gasped. Before he realized that he should let go of the gander's neck, he was so high up that he would have been killed instantly if he had fallen to the ground. All he could do was try to get on the gander's back and hold on for dear life. Staying on that slippery back was no simple matter, either, between two swaying wings. He had to dig deep into feathers and down with both hands to keep from falling.

The Big, Checked Cloth

The winds howled and beat against the gander and his small, unwilling companion; and to Nils, the rustle of feathers and swaying of wings sounded like a terrific storm. Thirteen geese flew around him, flapping their wings and honking. They danced before his eyes and buzzed in his ears until he was giddy.

He did not know whether they were flying high or low, or even in which direction they were traveling. After a bit, he regained enough sense to understand that he ought to find out where the geese were taking him. But he didn't dare to look down for fear that he might faint. Actually, the wild geese were not flying very high because the white gander could not breathe in the very thinnest air. For his sake they also flew a little slower than usual.

At last Nils glanced down at the ground. "How different everything looks from the air!" he thought. "Why, the ground looks like a great big carpet with an incredible number of large and small checks. Where in the world am I now?" He saw nothing but checks upon checks. Some were broad and ran crosswise,

and some were long and narrow. All over, there were angles and corners. Nothing was round, and nothing was crooked.

"What kind of a big, checked cloth is this that I'm looking down on?" he said to himself without expecting an answer. But instantly the wild geese who flew about him called out, "Fields and meadows. Fields and meadows." Then Nils realized that the big, checked cloth he was traveling over was the flat land of southern Sweden, and he began to comprehend why it was so checked and multicolored.

The bright-green checks were rye fields that had been sown in the fall and had remained green under the winter snows. The yellowish-gray checks were stubble fields—what was left of the oat crop that had grown there the summer before. The brownish checks were old clover meadows, and the black ones were deserted grazing lands or ploughed fallow pastures. The brown checks with the yellow edges were, without a doubt, beech-tree forests; because in the heart of a beech forest, you will find the big trees that are naked and dark in the winter, while the little beech trees along their borders keep their dry, yellowed leaves way into the spring.

The dark checks with gray centers were the large, built-up estates encircled by the small cottages with their blackening straw roofs and stone-divided plots of land. And then there were checks green in the middle with brown borders; these were the orchards, where the grass was already turning green although the trees and bushes around them were still in their nude, brown bark.

Nils could not keep from laughing when he saw how checked everything looked. But when the wild geese heard him, they called out reprovingly, "Fertile and good land. Fertile and good land."

Startled back into the reality of his remarkable situation, Nils moaned, "To think that I laughed when I'm in so much trouble!" And for a moment, he was pretty serious; but it was not long before he was laughing again.

Now that he had grown somewhat accustomed to the ride and the speed, so that he could think of something besides holding himself on the gander's back, he began to notice that the sky was full of birds flying north. The flocks called to one another. "So you came over today?" shrieked some. "Yes," answered the geese. "Do you think spring is here?" "Not yet. Not yet. Not a leaf on the trees. Ice-cold water in the lakes," came the answer.

When the geese flew over a place where they saw tame roosters and hens, they shouted, "What's the name of this place?

What's the name of this place?" Then the roosters cocked their heads and answered, "It's Lillgarde this year—the same as last year."

Most of the cottages were probably named after their owners, which is the custom in Skåne. But instead of saying, "This is Per Matsson's" or "Ola Bosson's," the roosters hit upon the kinds of names which, to their way of thinking, were more appropriate. Those who lived on small farms and belonged to poor cottages cried, "This place is called Grainscarce." And those who belonged to the poorest hut-dwellers screamed, "The name of this place is Little-to-Eat, Little-to-Eat." The big, well-cared-for farms got high-sounding names from the roosters—such as Luckymeadows, Eggberga and Moneyville.

The roosters on the great landed estates were too high and mighty to condescend to anything like joking. One of them crowed and called out with such gusto that it sounded as if he wanted to be heard way up to the sun: "This is Herr Dybeck's estate, the same this year as last year, this year as last year." Another strutting rooster crowed, "This is Swanholm. Why, everyone knows that!"

Nils was enjoying himself. This trip was not only teaching him more geography than he had learned in school (which was next to nothing), but it made learning fun! The geese, he saw, did not fly straight forward; but zigzagged over the whole south country, just as though they were glad to be in Skåne again and wanted to visit every single village and estate.

They went to one place where there were big, clumsy-looking buildings with tall chimneys, and all around these were a lot of small houses. "This is Jordberga Sugar Refinery," cried the roosters below. Nils felt a chill go down his back. He ought to have recognized this place, for it was not very far from his home. Why, last year he had worked at Jordberga Sugar Refinery as a watchman; but of course, nothing seen from the air looks exactly like it does from the ground.

And think! Just think about Osa the goose-girl and little Mats, who were his companions last year. What would they say if they suspected that he was flying over their heads! Nils would have liked to have seen them, but Jordberga was soon lost to sight. Along with the wild geese and his white goosey-gander, Nils traveled toward Svedala and Skaber Lake and back again over Görringe Cloister and Häckeberga. Nils saw more of Skåne in this one day than he had ever seen in all his life.

Whenever the wild geese happened to spot any tame geese, they had the best fun! The flew forward very slowly and called down, "We're off to the hills. Are you coming along? Are you coming along?" But the tame geese answered, "It's still winter in this country. You are out too soon. Fly back! Fly back!"

The wild geese flew even lower, so they could be heard even better, and called, "Come along! We'll teach you how to fly

and swim." Then the tame geese felt insulted and wouldn't answer them with a single honk. The wild geese flew still lower, almost touching the ground. Then, quick as lightning, they raised up, just as if they had been terribly frightened. "Oh, oh, oh!" they exclaimed. "Those things were not geese. They were only sheep. They were only sheep." The tame geese on the ground were beside themselves with rage and shrieked, "May the hunters get you! May you be shot, all of you! All of you!"

Nils laughed at the teasing. Then he remembered the trouble he was in, and wept in despair. But, oh how funny the geese could be! The next second, he was laughing again.

Nils had never ridden so fast and recklessly, with the air so fresh and bracing, and with such a fine scent of soil rising from the tilled ground. Oh, how wonderful! He had never dreamed of riding so high above the earth. Why, it was like flying away from life's problems and sorrows. And this was only the beginning of his adventure in the magical kingdom of the wild geese.

THE TRAVELS OF
BOOK ONE
NILS HOLGERSSON

Chapter Two

Akka From Kebnekaise

Evening

The big, tame goosey-gander was proud that the wild geese permitted him to fly with them. He enjoyed traveling back and forth over the South country and cracking jokes with the tame birds on the ground below. But in spite of his keen delight in this new way of life, he began to tire as the afternoon wore on. He tried to take deeper breaths and quicker wing strokes, but he still remained several goose-lengths behind the others.

When the wild geese who flew last in the majestic angle noticed that the tame one could not keep up with them, they began to call to the goose who led the procession: "Akka from Kebnekaise! Akka from Kebnekaise!"

"What do you want?" asked the leader.

"The white one will be left behind; the white one will be left behind."

"Tell him it is easier to fly fast than slow," Akka called back, and raced on as before.

The goosey-gander tried desperately to follow the leader's advice, increasing his speed just a little; but then he became so exhausted that he sank way down to the drooping willows that bordered the fields and meadows.

"Akka, Akka, Akka from Kebnekaise!" cried the wild geese who were watching the goosey-gander's struggle.

"What do you want now?" the leader asked (and now she sounded angry).

"The white one sinks to the earth; the white one sinks to the earth."

"Tell him it is easier to fly high than low!" the leader shouted, and she raced on as before.

The poor goosey-gander wanted to follow her advice; but when he attempted to fly higher, he became so winded that he almost burst his breast. Oh, how his heart was pounding!

"Akka, Akka!" again cried the wild geese who flew last in line.

"Won't you let me fly in peace?" asked the leader, even angrier than before.

"The white one is about to collapse."

"Tell him that he who is not strong enough to fly with the flock can go back home!" cried the leader. She had no intention of decreasing her speed, and raced on as before.

"Ah, is that the way it is?" thought the goosey-gander, bitterly. Why, the wild geese had never intended to take him to Lapland with them. They had only lured him away from home in sport.

To think that his wings should fail him now! He wanted to show these tramps that even a tame goose had both courage and strength. But—and this was most provoking of all—the leader of this flock was no ordinary wild goose. Tame goose that he was, he had heard about a leader goose, named Akka, who was more than a hundred years old. She was so famous that the best wild geese in the world followed her. But no wild goose ever had such a contempt for tame geese as Akka and her distinguished flock; and if only he could, the goosey-gander gladly would have shown them that he was their equal.

He flew slowly behind the rest, wondering whether he should turn back or continue. Finally, the little tomten on his back said, "Dear Morten Goosey-Gander, you know very well that you are too weak to fly all the way to Lapland with the wild geese. Why, this is the first time you have ever been high off the ground! You had better turn back before you kill yourself."

Whether the tiny tomten was teasing him or not, the goosey-gander couldn't be sure. But the very thought that the puny little creature actually believed that he could not make the trip hurt his pride. Aching wings and a pounding heart were bad enough, but that was more than he could bear. "If you say another word about that, I will drop you into the first ditch we fly over!" he cried. At the same time, his fury pumped up so much adrenalin that he began to fly nearly as well as any of the wild geese.

Morton Goosey-Gander could not have kept this grueling pace for long, nor was it necessary; because just then, the sun sank; and at sunset, the geese flew down. Before the boy and the goosey gander knew what had happened, they stood on the shores of Vomb Lake.

"They probably intend to spend the night here," Nils thought, and he jumped down from the goosey-gander's back. He stood on the narrow beach by the lake. What he saw was not very comforting to a boy who was used to snuggling down in a warm bed at home. The lake was almost entirely covered with ice—black and uneven, and full of cracks and holes, as spring ice generally is.

The ice was already breaking up. Oh, that cold, cold ice! It was loose and floating in the dark, shining water; but there was enough left to spread chill and winter terror over the place.

Looking toward the other side of the lake, Nils could barely make out open country, still light under the last rays of sun. Where the geese had lighted, there was dense pine growth. The forest of firs and pines seemed to bind the winter to itself. Everywhere else the ground was bare; but beneath the sharp pine branches lay snow that had been melting and freezing, melting and freezing, until it was as hard as ice.

Nils was so miserable and discouraged that he wanted to scream. He was hungry, too. He hadn't eaten anything all day. Where would he find food, and who would give him shelter?

Who would protect him from wild animals?

The sun slipped below the horizon; and as darkness fell from heaven, a grim frost crept out over the land, and terror followed the last glimmer of twilight. Nils heard alarming sounds—patters and rustling in the forest. Such a big forest...and he so little.

For the first time, Nils realized how dependent he was upon his traveling companions. If it were not for them, he would be very, very alone. All the fun of his ride through the air over Sweden was forgotten in a moment. Nils looked around for the goosey-gander.

There he was, having even a worse time of it than the boy. He was lying prostrate on the spot where he had landed, looking as if he were about to die. His neck lay flat against the ground, his eyes were closed, and his breathing was no more than a feeble hissing.

"Oh, Morton Goosey-Gander," Nils pled, "try to get a few sips of water! The lake is only two steps away." But the gander did not stir.

Dreadfully afraid of losing the only source of companionship and protection he had left, Nils began to push and drag the big, heavy bird to the water's edge. Finally he succeeded. At first the gander lay motionless, head down in the icy water; but soon he revived, and he shook the water from his feathers. Morton Goosey-Gander sniffed in satisfaction, then swam imperiously between reeds and seaweed. "I showed them; I showed them!" he seemed to say.

The wild geese had not given either the tame goose or his tiny rider so much as a thought since they had landed, but had made straight for the water. They had bathed and primped, and now they gulped half-rotten pond weed and water clover.

The white goosey-gander had the good fortune to spy a perch. He caught it in his beak, swam ashore and laid it down in front of the boy. "Here is a small thank-you gift for helping me into the water," he said.

It was the first time Nils had heard a friendly word that day. He was so happy that he wanted to throw his arms around the goosey-gander's neck, but he refrained; and he was genuinely thankful for the fish...even though it was raw.

The boy felt to see if he still had his sheath knife with him; and, yes, it still hung on the back button of his trousers. The knife was very tiny—hardly the length of a match. Even so, Nils managed to scale and clean the perch. Cutting the fish into small pieces, he ate it. Oh, the flavor was so good; and how wonderful it was not to be hungry!

When the boy was finished, he felt a little strange because he had been able to eat raw fish. The thought struck him, "Now I must be a real tomten and not human at all."

The goosey-gander had been standing silently beside him. But when Nils had swallowed the last bite of fish, the gander whispered: "These wild geese despise tame birds."

"Yes, I've noticed that," said the boy.

"I'd like to follow them all the way to Lapland and show them that a tame goose can be just as brave, as smart, and as physically fit as any wild goose!"

"Y-e-e-s," said the boy, doubtfully. He didn't really think that Morton Goosey-Gander could ever fly that far, or fly fast enough to keep up with the experienced, flight-hardened wild geese. Yet, he did not want to contradict him.

"But I don't think I can get along without your help. Would you be willing to come with me?"

The boy, of course, had expected to go home; and he was so surprised that he didn't know what to say. "I...I thought you and I were enemies." But this the goosey-gander seemed to have forgotten; after all, the boy had saved his life.

"I suppose I really ought to go home to my father and mother," Nils said in a questioning voice.

"Oh! I'll get you back to them in the fall," replied the goosey-gander. "I won't leave you until I put you down on your own doorstep."

Nils thought it might be just as well for him if he didn't see his parents for a while. He was about to agree with the gander's plan when they heard a loud rumbling behind them. Startled, Nils and Morton Goosey-Gander turned around to look. The wild geese had flown up from the lake all at one time, and stood shaking the water from their backs. They arranged themselves in a long row, with the lead goose in the center, and came toward the two newcomers.

As Morton Goosey-Gander sized up the wild geese, he felt ill at ease. He had expected them to be more like tame geese. He had thought that he would have felt a kindred spirit with them. But he must have been wrong. They were much smaller than he, and not one of them was white; they were gray with a sprinkling of brown. He was almost afraid of their eyes; they were yellow and shone as if a fire had been kindled behind them.

That was not all that was different. The goosey-gander's mother had taught him to walk slowly, with a rolling motion. These strange creatures did not walk; why, they half ran. He was most alarmed when he saw their feet. They were large, and the soles were torn and ragged. The wild geese must never have questioned where they landed or what they tramped on. They were very neat and well cared for in other respects, but one could see by their feet that they were a poor wilderness flock.

The goosey-gander had only enough time to whisper, "Nils! Whatever you do, don't tell them your name!" before the geese were upon them.

When the wild geese stopped in front of the newcomers, they curtsied with their necks several times; and the goosey-gander responded in the same manner. As soon as the ceremony was over, the lead goose said, "Now I presume we shall hear what you have to say about yourselves."

"There isn't much to tell," said the goosey-gander. "I was born in Skanor last spring. In the fall I was sold to Holger Nilsson of West Vemminghög, and I have lived on his farm ever since then."

"You don't seem to have any pedigree to boast of," said the haughty leader. "Why do you have the audacity to think that you can associate with wild geese?"

Morton Goosey-Gander replied, "Perhaps to show you wild geese that tame birds might also be of merit."

"Oh? Well, we would certainly like to see you prove that,"

said Akka from Kebnekaise. "We have already observed how much you know about flying. Are you, perhaps, more skilled in other sports? Would you be a worthy contender in a swimming contest?"

"No, I am not a great swimmer," admitted the goosey-gander. Now almost positive that the lead goose would send him home, he said, "I've never swum any farther than across a marl ditch."

"Well then, I presume you are a crack sprinter," Akka suggested.

"Oh, no. I have never even seen a tame goose run, and I have never done any running myself," the goosey-gander replied.

To his and the boy's astonishment, Akka said, "Well... you answer questions bravely. The goose who has courage can become a good traveling companion, even if he is ignorant at first. Would you like to stay with us for a few days, long enough to show us what you can do?"

"Yes, I would! Yes, of course!" exclaimed the goosey-gander.

Then Akka from Kebnekaise pointed with her bill at the little tomten. "But who is that with you? I have never seen anything like him before." "He is a friend of mine," the goosey-gander replied. "He has tended geese all of his life, so he will be helpful on the trip."

"Is that right?" answered the wild one. "He may be able to help a tame goose. What do you call him?"

"He has several names," the goosey-gander said guardedly, afraid to admit that his friend had a human name. After a pause, he said, "I call him Thumbietot."

"Oh? Does he belong to the tomten family?"

The gander fumbled, "Uh...um...what time do you wild

geese retire for the night? My eyes close by themselves about this time."

During the conversation, Nils Holgersson (now Thumbietot) had been studying the lead goose. She was very old. Her feather outfit was ice gray, without any dark streaks. The head was larger, the legs were coarser, and the feet were more worn than any of the others. The feathers were stiff, the shoulders knotty, the neck thin. All of these were characteristics of age. But Akka's eyes had not dimmed with age! They shone brighter—as if they were younger—than any of the others!

"What? Did I hear you correctly? Your eyes have to close right now—now, while I am talking to you? Understand, Mr. Tame-goose, that I am Akka from Kebnekaise! The goose who flies nearest me, to the right, is Iksi from Vassijaure; and the one to the left is Kaksi from Nuolja! Understand also that the second right-hand goose is Kolmi from Sarjektjakko; and the second, left, is Neljä from Svappavaara; and behind them fly Viisi from Oviksfjällen and Kuusi from Sjangeli! And know that these, as well as the six goslings who fly last—three to the right and three to the left—are all high-mountain geese of the finest breed! You must not take us for land-locked geese who strike up a chance acquaintance with any and everyone! And you must not think that we permit anyone to share our quarters unless he names his ancestors."

Nils decided it was time to answer for himself. "Please listen to me. I will make no secret of who I am. My name is Nils Holgersson. I am a farmer's son; and until today, I have been a human being..." He got no further. At the word *human*, the lead goose had staggered back. In a moment, all of the wild geese surrounded Nils, hissing in anger.

"I suspected that ever since I first saw you," Akka said between hisses. "Go! And go now! We do not tolerate human beings among us!"

Showing even more boldness than before, Morton Goosey-Gander spoke up: "Is it possible that you wild geese are afraid of such a tiny person? He will go home tomorrow, but couldn't you allow him to stay with us overnight? How could anyone force such a defenseless little creature to wander off by himself in the night, among weasels and foxes?"

Akka peared closely at the boy, but her agitation was apparent. "I have learned to fear everything in human shape, big or little," she said. "But if you will be responsible for him and swear that he will not harm us, he can stay with us tonight. Our night quarters are not suitable for him, obviously. We intend to roost on the broken ice out there."

"She is wise who knows how to choose such a safe bed," the goosey-gander replied.

"Hmm. You, Tame One, will be answerable for his departure tomorrow."

"I must leave, too," said the goosey-gander, "because I have promised not to abandon him."

"You are free to leave, of course." The lead goose raised her wings and flew out over the ice; and one after another, the wild geese followed her.

Nils was despondent. All hope of flying with the wild geese was gone. He was a very tired boy…and cold. "We will freeze to death on the ice," he murmured.

"There's no danger of that, my little friend," said the goosey-gander. "Gather as much dry grass and litter as you can." A little more cheerfully, Nils obediently ran along the shore, picking up bunches of dry grass and weeds. When his arms and pockets were full, he returned to the patient white goose.

"Hang onto the grass, Thumbietot, and I'll hang onto you." Grabbing the boy's shirtband in his bill, the goosey-gander lifted him and flew out on the ice, where the wild geese were already fast asleep, their bills tucked under their wings.

"Now spread the grass on the ice, so when I stand on it, my feet won't freeze fast."

Nils again did as he was told. When he had finished, the boy asked, "But where will I sleep?"

The goosey-gander gently picked him up by the shirtband and tucked him under his wing. "I think you'll be snug and warm there."

Nils was so covered by goosedown that he couldn't answer; and he was oh, so comfortable. And he was oh, so tired! And in less than two winks, he was sound asleep.

Night

Spring ice is treacherous, shifting with the wind and current. In the middle of the night, the loosened sheet of ice on Vomb Lake moved until one corner of it touched the shore. Now it happened that Smirre Fox, who lived in Övid Cloister Park on the east side of the lake, caught a glimpse of that one corner while he was out on his night chase. Smirre had seen the wild geese early in the evening, never supposing that he might catch one of them; but now he walked right out on the ice.

Just as Smirre was ready to pounce upon a sleeping goose, his claws scraped the ice. The geese awoke, flapped their wings and prepared for flight. But Smirre was too quick for them. He darted forward, grabbed a goose by the wing, and scrambled toward land.

Oh, but Smirre Fox had not accounted for a human being among the geese! The boy had awakened when Morton Goosey-Gander spread his wings. He had tumbled down onto the ice and was sitting there, dazed. He hadn't grasped the reason for all the consternation until he caught sight of a little, long-legged dog running across the ice with a goose in his mouth.

Without thinking, Nils ran after the thief and his prey. He must have heard the goosey-gander calling: "Be careful, Thumbietot! Be careful!" But the boy only wondered, "Why should anyone be afraid of such a runt of a dog?"

The wild goose in Smirre's jaws heard the clatter of Nils' wooden shoes on the ice. "Does that infant think he can rescue me?" And in spite of her predicament, she began to cackle in laughter. "Why, before he knows what has happened, he will have fallen through a crack in the ice!"

But dark as the night was, the boy saw all of the cracks and holes, and nimbly jumped over them. Under the old tomten's spell, he had the supernatural eyesight of the tomten and could see in the dark. Why, he could see both the lake and the shore just as clearly as if he were in broad daylight!

Smirre Fox had managed to get the goose onto shore. And just as he was working up the shoreline to the edge of the forest, the boy shouted: "Drop that goose!" Smirre heard Nils; but instead of looking around to see who was chasing him, he ran faster.

Pride getting the best of him, all Nils could think about was the contemptuous way in which he had been received by the wild geese. He was determined to prove that human beings were superior to animals of any kind. He shouted, "What kind of a dog are you? How dare you steal a goose! Drop her, or you'll get a beating you'll never forget! Drop her, or I'll tell your master what you've done!"

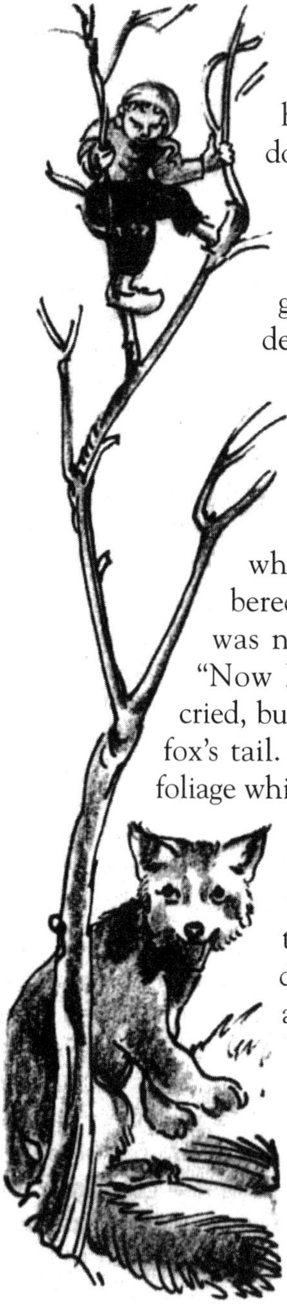

When Smirre Fox realized that he had been mistaken for a farm dog, he was so amused that he nearly did drop the goose. Smirre was notorious for his plundering. In his district, he was even feared. No, he wasn't satisfied to hunt rats and pigeons in the fields. He even ventured into farmyards to steal chickens and geese.

Nils finally caught up with him; but when he grabbed Smirre's tail, he remembered (quick as a flash, but too late) that he was no bigger, nor stronger, than a tomten. "Now I'll take the goose away from you!" he cried, but he had all he could do to hang onto the fox's tail. Smirre dragged him along until the dry foliage whirled around him.

Before long, Smirre stopped short and took a closer look at the tiny creature gripping his tail. Snickering, he put the goose on the ground and held her down with his forepaws so she couldn't fly away. He was ready to bite off her neck, but he couldn't resist the desire to tease the tomten a little. "Hurry off and complain to the master, because I'm about to eat this nice, fat goose!"

Stung by his contempt, Nils took a firmer hold on the tail and braced himself against a beech trunk. Just as the fox was about to clamp his jaws on the goose's throat, Nils pulled as hard as he could. Smirre was so astonished that he lost his grip, and the wild goose got away. She feebly fluttered upward. One wing was so badly wounded that she could barely use it. She was out of the fox's range; but because she could not see well in the dark, she could not help her rescuer. So, she groped her way through the branches and flew down to the lake, leaving him to his fate.

"If I can't have the goose, I'll have you, Mr. Tomten!" "Oh, do you think so?" Nils replied. He was in the best of spirits because he had saved the goose. But the boy was wise enough to know that hanging onto the fox's tail was far safer than letting go and feeling his sharp teeth!

There was such a dance in that forest that the dry beech leaves flew! Smirre swung round and round; but his tail swung too, so he could not grab the boy. Fearing that the cunning fox would eventually get him, Nils let go of the tail and climbed up a slender beech tree. From high above, he watched the fox spin in circles, trying in vain to catch his tail.

If only Nils had thought before he opened his mouth this time! But he didn't. "Don't bother with the dance anymore, Foxy!"

Smirre stopped and looked up. With a satisfied bark, he stretched out under the tree to wait for the tiny tot to lose his hold and fall down, into his waiting jaws. Nils was sitting on a little branch, one just strong enough to hold him if he didn't move. Looking around, he realized that he couldn't reach another tree, and he didn't dare climb down. He was so cold and numb that he could hardly hang on; and he was so awfully tired...

But he hung on...and on...and on. How awful—to sit that way the whole night! Nils had never understood the real meaning of "night." It was as if the whole world had become petrified and would never come to life again.

Dawn finally erased the blackness, and everything began to look more like itself once more, although the chill was even sharper than it had been during the night.

The sun came up red, not yellow. Nils wondered why. Was the sun angry because the night had made the earth so cold and gloomy?

Sunbeams rushed down in sparkling clusters to see what the night had been up to. The clouds in the skies, the satiny beech limbs, the intertwined branches of the forest canopy, the hoarfrost that covered the foliage on the ground—everything grew flushed and red as if with a guilty conscience.

More and more sunbeams came bursting through space, and soon the night's terrors were driven away. A black woodpecker, with a red neck, began to hammer with its bill on a branch. A squirrel glided from his nest with a nut, and sat down on a branch and began to shell it. A starling came flying with a worm, and a bullfinch sang high up in a tree.

Then, like a tomten, the boy understood. The sun had said to all these tiny creatures: "Wake up now, and come out of your nests. You don't need to be afraid of anything as long as I am here!"

The wild geese were awake, too. Nils heard them call from the lake, as they were preparing for the flight to Lapland. The boy tried to call to them, but they flew so high that his voice could not reach them. They probably believed that the fox had eaten him, and they didn't trouble themselves to look for him.

Nils would have cried; but the big, orange-colored orb put courage into the boy's heart, too. As it had said to all the wild things, the sun said to him: "It isn't worthwhile, Nils Holgersson, for you to worry about anything as long as I'm here."

Goose-Play

Monday, March twenty-first.

Everything remained unchanged in the forest—about as long as it takes a goose to eat her breakfast. But just as the morning was verging on noon, a goose came flying, all by herself, under the thick canopy of trees. She groped her way hesitatingly, between the stems and branches, and flew very slowly. As soon as Smirre Fox saw her, he left his place under the beech tree, and sneaked toward her. To his surprise, the wild goose didn't avoid him, but actually flew close to him. Smirre made a high jump for her but missed her, and the goose flew on down to the lake.

Before long, another goose came flying. She took the same route as the first one, and flew still lower and slower. She, too, flew close to Smirre Fox; and he made such a high spring for her that his ears brushed her feet. But she got away from him unhurt and went her way toward the lake, silent as a shadow.

A little while passed, and then there came another wild goose. She flew still slower and lower, and it seemed even more difficult for her to find her way between the beech branches. Smirre made a powerful spring! He was within a hair's breadth of catching her, but that goose also managed to save herself.

After she had disappeared, a fourth goose appeared. She flew so slowly and so badly that Smirre Fox thought he could catch her without much effort, but he was afraid of failure now and let her fly by. She took the same direction the others had taken; and just as she was right above Smirre, she sank down so far that he was tempted to jump for her. He jumped so high that he touched her with his tail; but she quickly flung herself to one side, saving her life.

Before Smirre could catch his breath, three more geese came flying in a row. They flew just like the rest, and Smirre made high springs for them all; but he did not succeed in catching a single goose.

After that came five geese, but these flew better than the others. And although it seemed that they wanted to lure Smirre to jump, he controlled his urge to fall into their trap. After quite a long time, a single goose came—the thirteenth. She was so old that she was gray all over, without a dark speck anywhere on her body. One wing seemed to be broken, and she flew so erratically that sometimes she almost touched the ground. Smirre went wild. This goose could not escape, he thought. Smirre jumped not only once; why, he went running and jumping after her all the way down to the lake. But he didn't catch her.

A fourteenth goose came flying. Ah, this one was a beauty! All white, its great wings swaying gracefully in even, steady strokes, it glistened like a bright light in the dark forest. When

Smirre Fox saw this one, he jumped halfway up the tree canopy. But the white one avoided him with no effort at all.

Suddenly Smirre remembered his prisoner in the beech tree. Just as he might have expected, the boy had disappeared. Smirre howled in rage!

But he didn't have much time to think about the boy, because now the first goose came back from the lake and flew slowly under the canopy. In spite of his frustration, Smirre was glad to see her. He darted after her. But he had been in too much of a hurry, and hadn't taken the time to calculate the distance, and he landed off the mark.

Then there came another goose; then a third, a fourth, a fifth, and so on. Finally the mighty angle of wild geese closed in with the icy-gray one and the big white one. They all flew low and slowly. Sinking down toward Smirre Fox, they seemed to invite him to try and catch them. Smirre lost all control.

The wild geese kept flying over his head. They came and went, came and went. Splendid geese, grown fat on the German heaths and grain fields, swayed all day through the woods, and so close to him that he touched them many times; yet he was not permitted to appease his hunger with a single one of them.

The winter was hardly gone yet, and Smirre recalled nights and days when he had been forced to tramp around in idleness, with not so much as a hare to hunt; when the rats hid themselves under the frozen earth; and when the chickens were all shut up. But all the winter's hunger had not been as hard to endure as this day's miscalculations.

Smirre was no young fox. He had had the dogs after him many a time, and had heard the bullets whizzing around his ears. He had lain in hiding, down in his lair, while the dachshunds crept into the crevices and all but found him. But all the anguish that Smirre Fox had been forced to suffer in that hot chase could not be compared with what he suffered every time he missed one of the wild geese.

In the morning, when the play had first begun, Smirre Fox had looked so stunning that the geese were amazed when they saw him. His coat was a brilliant red, his breast white, his nose black, and his tail as bushy as a plume. But by late afternoon, he was bathed in sweat; his eyes were dull; his tongue hung out; and froth oozed from his gaping jaws.

Smirre was so exhausted that he grew delirious. He saw nothing except flying geese. He made leaps for sun spots which he saw on the ground, and for a poor little butterfly that had come out of his chrysalis too soon.

The wild geese tormented Smirre unceasingly. They felt no compassion although they knew that Smirre was fevered and out of his head. When Smirre finally sank down on a pile of dry leaves, weak and defenseless, and next to death, they shouted in his ear: "Now you know, Mr. Fox, what happens to the one who dares to come near Akka of Kebnekaise!" With that they left him alone.

THE TRAVELS OF
BOOK ONE
NILS HOLGERSSON

Chapter Three

The Wonderful Journey of Nils

On the farm

Thursday, March twenty-fourth.

Just at that time something happened in Skåne which created a good deal of discussion and even got into the newspapers. Was the story true? Some thought so, and others refused to believe it. There was simply no practical explanation.

It was about like this: A lady squirrel had been captured in the hazelbrush that grew on the shores of Vomb Lake, and was carried to a farmhouse nearby. The people there were delighted with the pretty creature with the bushy tail; with the wise, inquisitive eyes and the cute little paws. They intended to amuse themselves all summer by watching it play.

So, they took an old squirrel cage from storage and cleaned it up. The cage had a little green house, with doors and windows, which the lady squirrel was to use as a dining room and bedroom. A cylinder wheel was placed in the cage so the squirrel could run and climb and swing around.

Everyone thought the little creature would be quite content, and they were disappointed because she sat forlornly in a corner of her room. Every now and then, she would let out a shrill, agonized cry. She refused to eat, and not once did she swing around on the wheel.

"It's probably because she is frightened," the people said. "She'll feel better tomorrow."

Meanwhile, the women on the farm were preparing for a feast. On that particular day, they were baking. They had bad luck with something; either the dough wouldn't rise properly, or they had been talking faster than they were working, because they had to work long after dark.

No one took time to think about the squirrel; that is, except for an old grandmother who was too old to help with the baking. Not wanting to go to bed yet, she sat down by the sitting-room window and looked out.

The kitchen door was open on account of the heat, and through it a clear ray of light streamed out into the yard. Why, the light was so bright that the grandmother could see all the cracks and holes in the plaster on the opposite wall. Then, little pattering sounds drew her attention to the squirrel cage.

In the bright light, the squirrel was running from her room to the wheel, and from the wheel to her room, without stopping an instant. The grandmother thought that was strange. Why should the squirrel be so nervous and active tonight? Maybe the bright lights from the kitchen were keeping the little animal awake.

Between the cowhouse and the stable there was a broad, handsome carriage gate; this too came within the light's radius. As the night wore on, the old grandmother saw a tiny creature, no bigger than a man's hand, cautiously steal his way through the gate. He was dressed in leather breeches and wooden shoes like any other working man. The grandmother knew at once that it was the tomten, and she was not the least bit frightened. She had always heard that the tomten was somewhere on the farm, although she had never seen him before; and the tomten brought good luck wherever he appeared.

As soon as the tomten came into the stone-paved yard, he ran up to the squirrel cage. Since it hung so high that he could not reach it, he went over to the storehouse to get a rod. When he came back, he leaned it against the cage. Then he quickly shinnied up the rod.

When he reached the cage, he shook the door of the little green house as if he wanted to open it; but the grandmother didn't move. She knew that the children had put a padlock on the door so the boys from the neighboring farms couldn't steal the squirrel. The old woman saw that when the tomten could not get the door open, the lady squirrel came out to the wire wheel. There they talked for a long time. When the tomten had heard all the imprisoned animal had to say to him, he slid down the rod to the ground and ran out through the carriage gate.

The grandmother didn't expect to see anything more of the tomten that night, but she remained at the window. After a few moments, he returned. He was in such a hurry that it seemed to her as though his feet hardly touched the ground. The old woman, with her farsighted eyes, saw him distinctly; and she also saw that he was carrying something, but what it was she couldn't imagine.

He laid one thing, which he had been carrying under his left arm, down on the pavement. He took another thing with him to the cage. He kicked in a window and handed the mysterious something to the lady squirrel. Then he slid down the rod and picked up the thing he had left on the pavement. He took that up to the lady squirrel, too. Again he slid down the rod and ran out of the farmhouse. He was so fast that the old woman could hardly follow him with her eyes.

By now she was too excited to sit still in the house. She very slowly and quietly went out to the backyard and waited by the pump to see if the little tomten would return.

Someone else had seen him, too. This was the house cat. He crept along slyly and stopped close to the wall, just a few inches from the stream of light.

Both the grandmother and the cat stood and waited, long and patiently, on that chilly March night. The old woman was just beginning to think about going in again when she heard a clatter on the pavement and saw the little tomten come trotting once more, carrying something under each arm. The burdens he bore squealed and squirmed. And now the grandmother understood what was happening. The tomten had hurried down to the hazel grove and brought back the lady squirrel's babies. He was carrying them to her so they wouldn't starve to death.

The old grandmother stood very still, hoping not to disturb them; and she didn't think the tomten had noticed her. He was about to lay one of the babies on the ground (so he could swing himself up to the cage with the other one) when he saw the house cat's green eyes glisten. He stood there, bewildered, with a young one in each hand.

He turned around and looked in every direction. Then he became aware of the grandmother's presence. Immediately he walked toward her, stretching his arms as high as he could reach, for her to take one of the baby squirrels.

The grandmother did not wish to prove herself unworthy of his trust, so she bent down and took the baby squirrel, and held it until the tomten had shinnied up to the cage with the other one. Then he came back for the one he had entrusted to her care.

The next morning, when the farm people had gathered together for breakfast, it was impossible for the old woman to keep from telling them what she had seen the night before. They all laughed at her, of course, and said that she had been dreaming. There were no baby squirrels this early in the year.

But she begged them to look in the squirrel cage, and they did to please her. There on the bed of leaves lay four tiny half-naked, half-blind baby squirrels, who were at least two days old.

When the farmer himself saw the young ones, he said: "One thing is certain. We should be ashamed." He took the mother squirrel and all her young ones from the cage and laid them in the old grandmother's lap. "Take these poor little creatures out to the hazel grove and give them their freedom!"

This was the story that people were talking about, and it had even gotten into the newspapers. Most people wouldn't believe it, though. How could anything like that have happened?

Vittskövle

Saturday, March twenty-sixth.

Two days later, another strange thing happened. A flock of wild geese landed on a meadow down in Eastern Skåne, not far from Vittskövle manor and very near the Eastern Sea. In the flock were thirteen wild geese of the usual gray variety and one white goosey-gander, who carried on his back a tiny boy dressed in yellow leather breeches, green vest, and white woollen toboggan hood.

After the wild geese had been feeding awhile, two children came along and walked along the edge of the meadow. The goose who was on guard at once rose into the air with noisy wing strokes, so that the whole flock knew there was danger. All the wild geese flew up; but the white goose waddled along on the ground, unconcerned. When he saw the others fly, he called after them: "You don't need to be afraid. They're children! They won't harm you."

The little creature, who had been riding on his back, trotted to the edge of the meadow, to the outskirts of a large, planted pine woods. He sat down on a knoll and picked a pine cone in pieces to get at the seeds.

When he saw the children, they were so close to him that he did not dare to run across the meadow to the goosey-gander. He hid under a dry thistle leaf and called a warning to the goose. But Morton Goosey-Gander had evidently made up his mind not to let himself be scared. Not once did he look up to see where the children were going.

Meanwhile, they walked across the field, getting nearer and nearer to the white goose. When he finally did look up, they were only a few feet away from him. Alarmed, he became so confused that he forgot he could fly, and tried to get out of their reach by running. But the children followed, chasing him into a ditch, and there they caught him. The larger of the two children tucked Morton Goosey-Gander securely under his arm and carried him off.

When the boy who lay under the thistle leaf saw this, he jumped up as if he intended to take the goose away from them. Then he must have remembered how little and powerless he was, because he threw himself on the knoll and beat the ground with his clenched fists.

Morton Goosey-Gander cried: "Thumbietot, come and help me! Oh, Thumbietot, come and help me!"

Nils laughed grimly. "Oh, yes! I'm just the one to help, I am!" But he got up and followed the goosey-gander. "At least I can find out where they are taking him," he thought.

The children had a good start, but the boy had no difficulty in keeping up with them until they came to a hollow where a brook hindered him. He had to run alongside it until he could find a place narrow enough for him to jump over.

By then the children had disappeared; but Nils could see their footprints on a narrow path leading into the woods, and he followed them. Soon he came to a crossroad. Here the children must have separated, because there were footprints in two directions.

Nils sighed. Then he saw a little white goosedown on a heather knoll, and he realized that the goosey-gander had dropped this pinch of under plumage to show him the way to go. Watching for more goosedown, and seeing traces here and there, Nils followed the children through the pine woods, across a couple of meadows, up on a road, and finally into a broad alley. At the end of the alley there was a great manor with gables and towers of red tile, decorated with bright borders and artistic designs.

"Maybe the children brought the goosey-gander here to sell him. By this time he's probably been butchered," Nils thought. But he wanted to know for sure, so he ran down the alley to the manor. Fortunately he met no one, for the tiny folk have good reason to be wary of being seen by human beings.

The mansion he came to was a splendid old structure with four great wings which enclosed a courtyard. On the east wing, there was a high arch leading into the courtyard. Nils went through the arch and into the courtyard, but there he stopped.

He was standing, his finger on his nose, thinking, when he

heard footsteps behind him. As he turned around to look, he saw about twenty young high-school students and their teacher out on a walking tour. Nils crept behind a water barrel near the arch.

When the students reached the arch, the teacher asked them to wait there a moment while he went in and asked for permission to tour the old castle of Vittskövle.

After the teacher left, one of the students went over to the water barrel and stooped down to drink. He had a tin box (such as botanists use) hanging around his neck. The box was in his way, evidently, so he threw it down on the ground. The lid flew open, and one could see that there were a few spring flowers in it.

The botanist's box had dropped right in front of the tomten, and the little creature must have thought that here was his best chance of getting into the castle and finding the goosey-gander. Nils smuggled himself into the box and hid under the anemones and colt's foot. Then the student picked the box up, hung it around his neck again, and closed the cover.

When the teacher returned, he announced that the group had been given permission to enter the castle. At first he led them to the courtyard, where he stopped and began to describe this ancient structure.

He called their attention to the first human beings who had inhabited this country, and who had been forced to live in mountain grottoes and caves, in the dens of wild animals, and in the brushwood; and that a very long period had elapsed before they learned to build huts from the trunks of trees. Another long period of time had gone by before they advanced from the log cabin, with its single room, to the building of a castle with a hundred rooms—like Vittskövle.

"About three hundred fifty years ago the rich and powerful built fortified castles like this one for themselves," he said. Vittskövle was erected at a time when wars and robbers made life in Skåne very unsafe. In those days there was a deep, wide moat all around the castle; and the moat was filled with water. The only way to get in or out of the castle was by crossing a drawbridge.

"Even to this day," the teacher continued, "there is a watchtower above the entrance gate. All along the sides of the castle there are long, narrow passageways that were once manned by sentries. Standing in the corners are high towers with walls nearly forty inches thick.

"Yet this castle was not built in the most savage era of war. Jens Brahe, who constructed it, had made it more than big, strong and secure; he had made it beautiful and comfortable.

"If you," he said, addressing his students, "could see the solid stone structure at Glimminge, which was built only a generation earlier, you would see that Jans Holgersen Ulfstand, the builder, was solely concerned about defensive fortification—not about aesthetic appeal, nor the comfort of the castle's inhabitants! Other castles, such as Marsvinsholm, Snogeholm and Övid's Cloister (which were erected one hundred years later), were magnificent homes. The gentlemen who built these places did not furnish them with any fortifications at all."

Nils was impatient; but he couldn't do anything about it, and he had to lie very still in the tin box. Finally the tour group went into the castle. But if Nils had hoped for a chance to crawl out of that box, he was wrong; and the teacher stopped every other minute to explain and instruct the students.

In one room he found an old fireplace, and that prompted him to talk about different kinds of fireplaces. The first indoor fireplace had been a big, flat stone on the floor of a hut, with an opening in the roof which let in both wind and rain. The next had been a stone hearth with no opening in the roof, making the hut warm enough but filled with soot and smoke. When Vittskövle was built, the architect had designed an open fireplace with a wide chimney for the smoke; but most of the warmth went up the chimney.

By now Nils had lain perfectly still for an hour. The teacher didn't hurry himself; but then he did not know that a poor little tomten lay shut up in a botanist's box, waiting for him to get through.

When he came to a room with gilded leather hangings, the teacher talked about the way people had decorated their walls and ceilings ever since the beginning of time. And when he came to an old family portrait, he talked all about historical changes in dress. In the banquet hall he described ancient wedding celebrations and funeral customs.

Then the teacher talked a little about the people who had lived in the castle: about the Brahes and Barnekows—about Christian Barnekow, who had given his horse to the king to help him escape; about Margareta Ascheberg who had been married to Kjell Barnekow and who, when a widow, had managed the estates and the whole district for fifty-three years; about banker Hageman, a farmer's son from Vittskövle, who had grown so rich that he had bought the entire estate; about the Stjernsvärds, who had given the people of Skåne better plows, enabling them to get rid of the old wooden plows that three oxen were hardly able to drag.

During all this, the boy lay still. If he had ever shut the cellar door on his father or mother, now he understood how they had felt. It seemed that hours went by before the teacher finished his lecture.

At last the teacher led his students back to the courtyard. And there he talked about the endless effort to acquire tools and weapons, and clothes and houses. He said that Vittskövle was a milepost on time's highway. Here one could see how far people had advanced three hundred fifty years ago, and one could judge whether people had advanced any farther since their time.

Nils sat up with a start! The schoolboy was thirsty again and stole into the kitchen to ask for a drink of water. When Nils was carried into the kitchen, he tried to look around for the goosey-gander. But as soon as he moved, he happened to press against the lid of the tin box. It flew open. Without thinking about it, the student shut it again. Then the cook asked him if he had a snake in the box.

"No, only some plants," the student replied.

"Something moved in that box!" the cook insisted, so the young man lifted the cover to show her that she was mistaken.

"See for yourself if..."

He got no farther. Quick as quick could be, the little tomten bounded onto the floor and scurried out of the kitchen into the courtyard. The maids hadn't gotten a good look at him, so they didn't know what he was; but they hurried after him anyway.

The teacher was still lecturing when he was rudely interrupted. "Catch him, catch him!" shrieked the cook, maids and schoolboy; and the high-school students raced after the little tomten. They tried to intercept him at the gate; but it was hard to capture such a quick little thing, and he escaped. Nils did not dare to go down the open alley, but ran through the garden into the backyard. By now a whole crowd of people was hounding the poor little creature who was running helter-skelter for his life.

As he rushed past a laborer's cottage, he heard a goose cackle, and saw a bit of white goosedown on the doorstep. The goosey-gander! Nils climbed up the steps and into the hallway. He couldn't get any farther, because the door was locked. He heard Morton Goosey-Gander moaning inside, but he couldn't get the door open. Nils' hunters were coming nearer and nearer; and in the room, the goosey-gander was crying more and more pitifully.

The boy pounded on the door as hard as he could. A child opened it, and Nils looked into the room. A woman was holding the goosey-gander tight, about to clip his quill feathers. She wanted to keep him with her own geese; but oh, how the very thought of losing his freedom made Morton Goosey-Gander moan and squawk!

Luckily she hadn't started the clipping sooner. Only two quills had fallen to the floor when Nils startled her. As superstitious as a person could be, she believed he was Goanisse himself. In her terror, she dropped the shears, clasped her hands, and forgot to hold onto the goosey-gander.

Morton Goosey-Gander ran to the door, grabbed the boy by the neckband and carried him out with him. On the stoop he spread his wings and flew up in the air. At the same time, he made a graceful sweep with his neck and seated the boy on his smooth, downy neck.

Off they flew, while all of Vittskövle stared after them.

In Övid Cloister Park

All that day, when the wild geese tormented Smirre Fox, the boy slept in a deserted squirrel nest. When he awoke, along toward evening, he felt uneasy. Although the geese had rescued him, he thought sadly, "I'm more a hindrance than a help to anyone. Akka from Kebnekaise will soon send me home, and then I will have to face my mother and father." But when he looked around and saw the wild geese, who bathed and preened in Vomb Lake, not one of them said a word about his going. "They probably think the white goose is too tired to travel home with me tonight," Nils decided.

The next morning the geese were awake long before sunrise. Curiously enough, both Nils and the white goosey-gander were permitted to follow the wild ones on their morning tour. The boy couldn't comprehend why.

The wild geese traveled over Övid's Cloister estate, which was situated in a park east of the lake. The castle was very imposing, with its well-planned court surrounded by low walls and pavilions; its fine, old-fashioned garden with covered arbors, streams and fountains; its perfectly trimmed trees and bushes, and its evenly mown lawns with their beds of spring flowers.

So early in the morning, no human beings were around to see the wild geese. When the geese were fully assured of that, they flew low over the dog kennel and shouted: "What kind of a little hut is this? What kind of a little hut is this?"

The dog burst from his kennel, furiously angry, and barked: "Do you call this a hut? You tramps! Can't you see that this is a great stone castle? Can't you see the fine terraces, pretty walls and windows and doors it has, bow, wow, wow, wow? Don't you see the grounds, can't you see the garden, can't you see the conservatories, can't you see the marble statues?

"You call this a hut, do you? Do huts have parks with beech groves and hazel bushes and trailing vines and oak trees and firs and hunting grounds filled with game, wow, wow, wow?

"Do you call this a hut? Have you seen huts with so many outhouses around them that they look like a whole village? You must know a lot of huts that have their own church and their own parsonage; and that rule over the district and the peasant homes and the neighboring farms and barracks, wow, wow, wow?

"Do you call this a hut? To this hut belong the richest possessions in Skåne. You beggars! You can't see a bit of land, from

where you hang in the clouds, that does not obey commands from this hut, wow, wow, wow!"

All this the dog managed to bark out in one breath; and the wild geese flew back and forth over the estate, and listened to him until he was winded. But then they cried: "What are you so angry about? We didn't ask about the castle, you ignorant dog; we only wanted to know about your kennel!"

The boy laughed at their joke. Then a thought came to him. How many amusing things might he hear if the geese allowed him and Morton Goosey-Gander to travel with them through the whole country, all the way to Lapland!

The wild geese flew to one of the wide fields, east of the estate, to eat grass roots; and they breakfasted for hours. While he waited, the boy wandered in the enormous park bordering the field. He hunted up a beechnut grove and began to search for nuts that might still cling to the bushes. Again and again the thought of the trip came to him. He pictured to himself what a great time he would have. He would freeze and starve; that he knew, of course; but he would escape chores and schoolwork, too!

As he walked among the bushes, the old gray lead goose came up to him and asked if he had found anything edible. No, he hadn't, he said; and then she tried to help him. She couldn't find any nuts either, but she did find a couple of dried blossoms that hung on a brier bush. Like a real tomten, Nils ate the blossoms with relish. Then he wondered what his mother would say if she knew that he had lived on raw fish and old, winter-dried blossoms!

When the wild geese had finally eaten their fill, they flew off to the lake again, where they amused themselves with games until noon. The wild geese challenged the white goosey-gander to take part in all kinds of sports. They had swimming races, running races, and flying races with him. The big tame one did his best to hold his own, but the clever wild geese beat him every time. All the while, the boy sat on the goosey-gander's back and encouraged him, and had as much fun as the rest. They laughed and screamed and cackled, and it was remarkable that the people on the estate didn't hear them.

Finally tired of play, the wild geese flew out onto the ice and rested for a couple of hours. They spent the afternoon much the same way as the morning: first, feeding; then bathing and playing in the water near the ice's edge until sunset, when they immediately settled down to sleep.

"This is the life for me," thought the boy when he cuddled down under the gander's wing. "But tomorrow, I suppose I'll be sent home."

Dreamily he thought about a sometimes leisurely, sometimes exciting life among the wild geese. He would escape scoldings for being lazy. He could do practically anything he wanted to, and all he would have to worry about was finding something to eat. And now he needed so little to eat!

Nils wasn't afraid of anything except being sent home, but not even on Wednesday did the geese say anything to him about going. That day passed, and the boy was growing more and more content with the outdoor life. He thought he had the lovely Övid Cloister park all to himself, and he wasn't anxious to return to his parents' stuffy little cottage and the little patch of ground they called their own.

Thursday began like the other days; the geese fed on the broad meadows, and the boy hunted for food in the park. After awhile, Akka helped him find something to eat—a dry caraway herb that had kept all its tiny seeds intact. After he had finished eating, Akka said that she thought he ran around in the park too recklessly. She wondered if he knew how many enemies he had to guard against—he, who was so little. No, he didn't know, he said. Then Akka began to teach him, as she would a young fledgling.

Whenever he walked in the park, she said, he must look out for the fox and the marten. When he went to the lakeshore, he must think of the otters. As he sat on the stone wall, he must not forget the weasels, who could creep through the smallest holes. And if he wished to lie down and sleep on a pile of leaves, he must first find out if the adders were sleeping their winter sleep in the same pile. In the open fields, he should keep an eye out for hawks and buzzards, and for eagles and falcons that soared in the air. In the bramble bushes, he could be captured by the sparrow-hawks; magpies and crows were everywhere, and in these he mustn't place much confidence. As soon as it was dusk, he must listen for the owls, who flew with such soundless wing strokes that they could come upon him before he was aware of their presence.

When the boy realized that so many were after his life, he was overwhelmed. How could he possibly survive! He asked Akka what to do.

She told him to try to make friends with all the small animals in the woods and fields: with the squirrel folk and the hare family, with bullfinches and the titmice and woodpeckers and larks. If he were their friend, they would warn him against dangers, find hiding places for him, and protect him.

But later in the day, when attempting to profit from her counsel, Nils' reputation caught up with him. Sirle Squirrel said, "How can you expect anything from me—or the rest of the small animals, for that matter! Don't you think we know that you are Nils the goose-boy, who tore down the swallow's nest last year, crushed the starling's eggs, threw baby crows in the marl ditch, caught thrushes in snares, and put squirrels in cages? You'd better help yourself. Just be thankful if we don't form a league against you and drive you back to your own kind!"

That was just the sort of answer the boy would not have let go unpunished when he was Nils the goose-boy. But now he was only afraid that the wild geese would learn how wicked he had been. True, he could no longer do much harm; but, little as he was, he could have destroyed birds' nests and crushed their eggs if he'd wanted to. But he hadn't so much as pulled a feather from a goose wing or given anyone a rude answer. Every morning when he talked to Akka, he had always removed his cap and bowed.

Without a word of denial or protest, Nils turned from the angry squirrel and walked away, his head on his chest. Well, that was the evening he heard that Sirle Squirrel's wife had been stolen and that her children were starving to death. And we have already been told how well he succeeded.

When Nils went into the park on Friday, he heard the bullfinches singing of how Sirle Squirrel's wife had been carried away by cruel robbers and how Nils, the goose-boy, had risked his life among human beings to return the squirrel children to her.

"Who is so honored in Övid Cloister park now as Thumbietot," sang the bullfinch, "he whom all feared when he was Nils the goose-boy? Sirle Squirrel will give him nuts; the poor hares are going to play with him; the small wild animals will carry him on their backs and fly away with him when Smirre Fox approaches. The titmice are going to warn him against the hawk, and the finches and larks will sing of his valor."

Nils was certain the geese had heard the bullfinch's song, yet not a word did they say. Friday went by, and Saturday morning came. The ravenous, revenge-seeking Smirre Fox was on the prowl again.

When the wild geese landed in the meadows, he lay in wait for them, and chased them from one field to another, never allowing them to eat in peace. As a result, Akka flew with her flock several miles away, over Färs' plains and Linderödsosen's hills. They did not stop until they had arrived in the district of Vittskövle.

At Vittskövle the goosey-gander was stolen, and how that happened has already been told. If the boy had not done everything he could to help the gander, he would never have been heard of again.

On Saturday evening, as the boy returned to Vomb Lake with the goosey-gander, he felt proud of himself. Maybe he was worth something after all. Yet, though the wild geese praised him for his courage, they never said a word about his going home or staying with them for the trip to Lapland.

Sunday afternoon he sat in a fluffy osier bush, down by the lake, and blew on a reed pipe. Finches and bullfinches and starlings—as many as the bushes would hold—were singing songs that he tried to play. But the boy played so poorly that the feathers raised on the little music teachers, and they whistled and scolded, hopped and fluttered in exasperation. Their antics were so funny that the boy laughed until he dropped his pipe.

He began once again, and that went just as badly. Then all the little birds wailed: "Today you play even worse than usual, Thumbietot! You don't make one true note! Where are your thoughts, Thumbietot?"

"Oh, somewhere else," he replied; and this was true. He still did not know if he would remain with the wild geese. Suddenly he threw his pipe down and jumped from the bush. He had seen Akka and her flock coming toward him in a long row. Their dignified, military manner let him know that now, at last, he would know what the future held.

When they stopped, Akka addressed Nils: "I'm sure you've wondered why I have not thanked you for saving me from Smirre Fox, but I would rather thank by deeds than by words.

"So, I sent word to the tomten who bewitched you. At first he did not want to cure you; but I have sent message upon message to him, telling him how well you have conducted yourself among us. Finally he has relented. As soon as you return to your home, you will become a human being again."

Instead of shouting "Hurrah!" and throwing his cap into the air, or something of that nature, Nils stared miserably at his wooden shoes. He didn't say a word, but a tear ran down his cheek.

"What! Do you mean I haven't done enough for you?" asked Akka.

But the boy was thinking of the carefree days and good-natured bantering, of adventure and freedom and travel high above Sweden. He would miss all of this. Like a small child, he began to sob.

"I...I don't want to be human," he said. "I...I want to go with you to Lapland."

"The tomten is touchy," replied Akka. "I'm afraid that if you do not accept his offer now, you may not be able to coax him another time."

As long as he could remember, Nils had never cared for anyone—not his father and mother; not his school teachers; not his schoolmates; not even for the boys in his neighborhood. Because he had always been so self-centered, he was not lonely for anyone he used to know!

The only acquaintanceships he had, really, were with Osa the goose-girl, and little Mats—a couple of children who had tended geese in the fields, like himself. But he didn't particularly care about them either.

"I don't want to be human!" bawled the boy. "I want to go with you to Lapland. That's why I've been good for a whole week!"

"Well, I won't forbid you to accompany us as far as you like," Akka said, "but I think you had better go home. A day might come when you would regret your decision to stay with us."

"No," said the boy. "I have never been as well off as with you."

"Then, let it be as you wish."

"Thank you! Thank you!" shouted the boy.

THE TRAVELS OF
BOOK ONE
NILS HOLGERSSON

Chapter Four

Glimminge Castle

Black Rats and Gray Rats

In southeastern Skåne, on the plains not far from the sea, stands an ancient castle called Glimminge. It is a substantial stone house, and can be seen for miles around. No more than four stories high, the castle is so massive that an ordinary farmhouse on the same estate looks like a child's playhouse.

Because of the thick ceilings and partitions, there is little room in its interior for anything except walls. The stairs are narrow, the entrances are small, and the rooms are few. There are hardly any windows in the upper stories and none at all in the lower ones.

This castle, you see, was constructed during a period of war. Later, when peace was restored in Skåne, the people of Glimminge deserted the dark and cold stone halls. They were relieved to move into homes where light and air could penetrate!

Now, when Nils Holgersson traveled with the wild geese, there were no human beings in Glimminge Castle. Yet the castle was not without inhabitants. A pair of gray owls lived in the attic; bats hung in the secret passages; and an old cat lived in the kitchen. Every summer a pair of storks lived in a large nest on the roof. And down in the cellar, hundreds of black rats thrived on the grain stored there.

Rats are not held in high esteem by other animals, but the black rats at Glimminge Castle were an exception. They were mentioned with respect, because they had always shown valor in battle with their enemies and endurance in hard times.

For centuries, the black rats had owned Skåne and the whole country. They were in every cellar, in every attic, in pantries and stables and barns, in breweries and flour mills, in churches and castles—as a matter of fact, in every building. They had lived here since the beginning of time; now they were practically extinct.

People had not exterminated them, as you might have expected. No, they were conquered by animals of their own kind—the gray rats. Descendants of two poor immigrants who landed in Malmö from a Libyan sloop about a hundred years ago, the gray rats were starved vagrants who stuck close to the harbor, swam among the piles under the bridges, and ate garbage that was thrown into the water.

They stayed out of the city, which was ruled by the black rats.

Always living against the odds, the gray rats became cunning and ferocious. At the moment they were at the mercy of the black rats, but that was only because the grays were fewer in number. They became bolder as they multiplied.

At first they took over some condemned housing that the black rats had abandoned. They hunted for food in gutters and trash heaps, and made the most of the rubbish that the black rats did not consider fit for use. Within a few years, they began to drive the black rats out of Malmö. They stole their attics, cellars and storerooms, starved them out or bit them to death.

When Malmö was captured, the gray rats made an all-out attack on the whole country. It is almost impossible to comprehend why the black rats did not martial themselves into a great united front to neutralize the grays' advance before it was too late. But the black rats had grown complacent. They were so certain of their power that they did nothing at all.

The gray rats methodically took farm after farm, city after city. Glimminge Castle was the black rats' last citadel. Could it stand against the holocaust?

The old castle had such secure walls and so few rat passages that the black rats managed to defend themselves. Years passed and the struggle continued between the aggressors and the defenders; but these, the last of the black rats, were excellent warriors. They were alert, they fought without fear of death, and they survived.

Of course the black rats had been no better than the grays. They had been shunned every bit as much, and for good reason. They had tortured prisoners who were chained in castle dungeons, violated the dead, stolen the last turnip from the poor, bitten off the feet of sleeping geese, robbed eggs and chicks from the hens, and plundered the country in a thousand other ways. But since they had been pushed until their backs were against the wall, all of this had been forgotten; and no one could help but admire the fight-to-the-death spirit of this band of defenders.

The gray rats, in the courtyard outside, could have allowed the black rats to occupy this solitary castle in peace, since they controlled the rest of the country. But the gray rats considered it a matter of honor to destroy this last reminder of the age when the black rats reigned supreme. Those who knew the gray rats surmised the real reason: Glimminge Castle was used by humans for grain storage. Grain! Gray or black, the rats would kill for grain.

The Stork

Monday, March twenty-eighth.

Early one morning, the wild geese who were standing or sleeping on the ice in Vomb Lake were awakened by an announcement from the air. Cranes were calling: "Trirop, Trirop! Trianut, the crane, sends greetings to Akka, the wild goose, and her flock. Tomorrow will be the day of the great crane dance on Kullaberg."

Akka raised her head and answered at once: "Greetings and thanks! Greetings and thanks!"

The messengers flew on, and the wild geese heard them for a long while, calling out over every field and wooded hill: "Trianut sends greetings. Tomorrow will be the day of the great crane dance on Kullaberg!"

Some geese motioned to the white goosey-gander, and he waddled over to join them.

"You're fortunate," they said, "to be invited to attend the great crane dance on Kullaberg!"

"What's so special about a crane dance?" he asked.

"It's beyond your imagination!"

Akka interrupted them. "We must decide what to do with Thumbietot while we are at Kullaberg."

The tame gander objected, "We cannot leave him alone! If he must stay here, I will stay with him."

"No human being has ever been permitted to attend the Animals' Congress at Kullaberg, and I wouldn't dare to break the rule," Akka replied. "But we will discuss this later. This is feeding time."

She gave a signal, and the flock of wild geese rose into the air. They followed her to the swampy meadows a little south of Glimminge Castle and a long way from Vomb Lake (on account of Smirre Fox).

For the rest of the day, the boy sat on the shore of a small pond, and blew on reed pipes. He was disgusted because he wasn't included in the invitation to see the crane dance. And he was feeling sorry for himself, too.

"After all," he thought, "I gave up the chance to be human just so I could stay with the wild geese. I ought to be allowed to do whatever they do!

"I'll tell Akka what I think!"

But hours went by, and he didn't say a word. The boy actually had acquired a kind of respect for the old goose. He knew that he could not set his will against hers and get away with it.

On one side of the swampy meadow, where the geese fed, was a stone hedge. Toward evening when the boy finally had the courage to talk to Akka, he happened to glance at the stone hedge. Something caught his attention. What was it?

He uttered a little cry of surprise, and all the geese looked up and stared in the same direction. The round, gray stones in the hedge seemed to have grown legs. Rats! Gray rats! They swarmed over the entire stone hedge—a huge company on the march.

The boy had always been afraid of rats, even when he was a big, strong human being. Now two or three of them could overwhelm him in a moment. He shuddered as he stood and stared at them.

The wild geese felt the same aversion. When the rats were out of sight, the geese shook themselves as if their feathers had been spattered with mud.

"The gray rats are on the move!" said Iksi from Vassipaure. "A bad omen."

Nils thought this was a good time to tell Akka that he didn't want to stay behind, but he was prevented once again. Suddenly, a big bird landed beside her. You might have thought, if you'd seen this bird yourself, that he had borrowed body, neck and head from a little white goose. But he also had large black wings, long red legs, and a thick bill, which seemed too large for the little head and weighed it down until it gave him a sad and anxious expression.

Akka immediately straightened out the folds of her wings and curtsied several times as she approached the stork. She wasn't surprised to see him in Skåne so early in the spring, because she knew that the male stork flies ahead of the female to inspect the nest for winter damage. But Akka was surprised that he had sought her out, since storks prefer to associate with members of their own family.

"Is there anything wrong with your house, Herr Ermenrich?" she asked.

Well, it's true, every word of it: a stork cannot open his bill without complaining. But what made his message even more solemn and alarming was the difficulty he had in speaking at all. He stood for a long time and only clattered with his bill. When he finally got over the stuttering, his voice was hoarse and weak; but his words tumbled one over another in a sudden rush.

He grumbled about the nest, which was at the very top of Glimminge Castle; it had been destroyed by winter storms. If that weren't bad enough, he said, he couldn't get any food at Skåne, because the humans there had dug out his marshes and ruined his swamps. He might just as well leave the country and never return.

While the stork grumbled, Akka thought to herself: "If I had your advantages, Herr Ermenrich, I wouldn't complain. You have remained a free and wild bird, yet you are so favored by human beings that no one will fire a shot at you or steal an egg from your nest." To the stork she only remarked how surprised she would be if he were willing to move from Glimminge Castle; after all, storks had resided there ever since it was built.

As though he had just remembered his purpose for meeting with the venerable old goose, the stork paused for a moment.

"Did you see the gray rats marching toward Glimminge Castle?" he asked.

"Yes, I saw the horrid creatures! Why do you ask?"

Herr Ermenrich began to tell her about the valiant black rats who, for years, had defended the castle.

"But tonight Glimminge Castle will fall into the gray rats' power," he sighed.

"Why tonight especially?" Akka asked.

"Well, because nearly all the black rats went over to Kullaberg last night. They thought all of the animals would be there.

"But the gray rats have conspired to take over Glimminge while the black rats are away! They're mustering enough gray rats to storm the castle. Only a few old black rats, who are too feeble to go to Kullaberg, are left at the castle.

"Oh, why did this have to happen! I've lived at Glimminge in harmony with the black rats for so many years that I hate to think I will have to live there with their enemies."

Akka nodded. She understood that the stork had become so disturbed over the gray rats' intentions that he had sought her out. But displaying the fatalistic attitude of storks in general, he hadn't done anything to divert the disaster; he had only come to complain.

"Have you sent word to the black rats, Herr Ermenrich?" she asked.

"No. It's no use. The castle will be taken before they could return."

"Don't be so sure," Akka said. "I know an old wild goose, I do, who will do her best to prevent this outrage!"

The stork stared at her, amazed. Akka, after all, was not outfitted for battle. She had neither claws nor sharp beak; and besides that, she was a day bird. The gray rats would raid the castle after dark!

But Akka had made up her mind. She called Iksi from Vassijaure and ordered him to take the wild geese to Vomb Lake. When some in the flock objected to leaving her, Akka said: "It will be best for all of us if you obey me. I must fly to the big stone house; and if you follow me, the people in the area will be sure to see us and attempt to shoot us down. So, the only one I want to take with me is Thumbietot. He will be of great help to me because he has good eyesight and he can stay awake at night."

The boy, who was still offended because he was not invited to the crane dance, was about to refuse to help Akka. But he didn't have a chance to say anything. As soon as the stork saw him, he grabbed the boy and, quick as a flash, tossed him in the air. He performed this feat seven more times, while the boy shrieked and the geese shouted: "What are you trying to do, Herr Ermenrich? That's not a frog! That's a human being, Herr Ermenrich!"

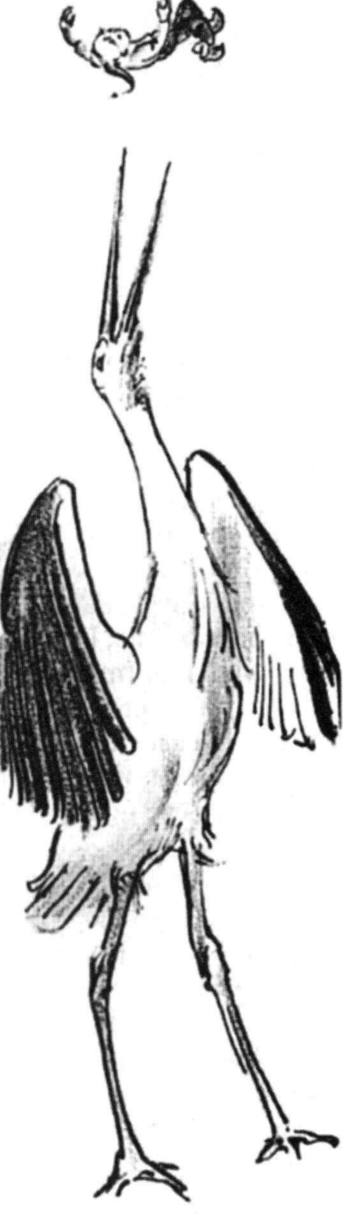

Finally the stork put the boy down entirely unhurt.

"I wondered what it was," he said, squinting at Nils, with a sparkle in his eye. Well, I'll fly back to Glimminge Castle now, Mother Akka. You'll be sure the animals who live there will be thrilled to know that you and the human tomten (he pointed with his bill at Nils) are on your way to rescue them."

The stork craned his neck, raised his wings, and darted off like an arrow when it leaves a well-drawn bow. Akka knew that he was making fun of her, but she didn't care. She waited until the boy had found his wooden shoes, which the stork had shaken off;

then she put him on her back and followed the stork.

Nils made no objection. He was so furious with the stork that he just sat and puffed. That long, red-legged thing thought he was a "nothing" just because he was little; but he would show him what kind of a man Nils Holgersson from West Vemminghög was.

Before long, Akka stood in the storks' nest. It had a wheel for a foundation, and the wheel was covered with grasses and twigs. The nest was so old that shrubs and plants had taken root in and around it. When the mother stork came and sat on her eggs, she would not only enjoy a scenic view of Skåne, but also the beautiful, wild brier blossoms and house leeks around her.

Both Akka and the boy saw something topsy-turvy, though. On the edge of the stork nest sat two gray owls, an old gray-streaked cat, and a dozen decrepit rats with protruding teeth and watery eyes. They were not exactly the combination of animals one would expect to coexist peaceably!

Not one of the animals welcomed Akka and her companion. They simply sat and stared at some long, gray lines, which came into sight here and there on the winter-naked meadows.

The black rats were silent, in deep despair, quite aware that they couldn't defend either themselves or the castle. The two owls rolled their big eyes and twisted their encircling eyebrows, talking in hollow, ghostlike voices about the awful cruelty of the gray rats; they said they would have to leave their nest because they had heard that the gray rats spared neither eggs nor baby birds. The old, gray-streaked cat was positive that the gray rats would bite him to death. He meowed, sheathed and unsheathed his claws, and scolded the black rats.

"How could you be so idiotic as to let your best fighters leave? How could you trust the gray rats? What you've done is unpardonable!"

The twelve black rats remained silent. But the stork, in spite of his own misery, could not refrain from teasing the cat.

"Don't worry so, Monsie Housecat! Can't you see that Mother Akka and Thumbietot have come to save the castle? Now I'm going to sleep, and I do so without a worry in the world.

Tomorrow there won't be a single gray rat in Glimminge Castle, will there, Mother Akka."

The boy winked at Akka and made a sign—as the stork stood at the very edge of the nest, with one leg drawn up, to sleep—that he wanted to push him down to the ground. But Akka restrained him. She did not seem to be angry. Instead she said confidently, "It'd be too bad if one as old as I am could not manage to get out of worse difficulties than this. If only Mr. and Mrs. Owl, who can stay awake at night, would fly off with a couple of messages for me, I think that we'll do just fine."

Both owls were willing to help. Akka asked the gentleman owl to tell the black rats at Kullaberg to hurry back. Then she asked the lady owl to fly to Flammea, the steeple owl, who lived in Lund Cathedral, with a commission so secret that Akka only dared to confide it to her in a whisper.

The Rat Charmer

It was getting on toward midnight when the gray rats succeeded in finding an open air hole in the cellar. The hole was high up on the wall; but the rats climbed up on one another's shoulders, and it wasn't long before the leader of the gray rats was sitting in the air hole.

She sat still for a moment, ready to force her way into the castle. She knew that most of the black rats had gone to Kullaberg, but she also knew that the rats who remained would not surrender without a struggle. With thumping heart she listened, but she didn't hear a sound. Then the leader of the gray rats plucked up courage and jumped down to the coal-black cellar.

One after another, the gray rats followed her. They all kept quiet, expecting at any moment to be ambushed by the black rats. Ever so careful, they wouldn't venture any farther into the castle until the cellar floor was teeming with gray rats.

Although they had not been inside the castle before, they had no difficulty finding their way. They located the passages in the walls that the black rats had used to get to the upper floors.

After they had stopped to listen attentively, they crept up to the first floor. They felt more frightened than if they had confronted the black rats immediately.

Oh, the scent of the grain! They could smell it now. It was stored in large bins on the floor. The gray rats wisely overcame their temptation to get into the grain. They searched, with the utmost caution, through the empty rooms. They ran up in the fireplace, which stood on the floor in the old castle kitchen; and they almost tumbled into the well, which was located in the inner room. Once the gray rats had stationed enough of their troops on the first floor, they went to the second floor.

Then, with the same caution, they began a bold and dangerous climb through the walls. The gray rats were breathless with anxiety, sure that they would be assaulted by the enemy at some point; and they were, oh, so tempted by the delicious odors from the grain bins! But they were disciplined rats. Ignoring both fear and temptation, they systematically inspected the ancient warriors' pillar-propped kitchen; their stone table and fireplace; the windows hollowed out of the thick walls; and the hole in the floor, which in days long past had been opened to pour boiling pitch on the enemy below.

Not a black rat was to be seen. The gray ones groped their way to the third story and into the lord of the castle's great banquet hall. The hall was cold and empty like all the other rooms in the old house. The rats climbed to the upper story, which had been a single room; and that, too, was barren.

The only place they did not think of exploring was the big stork nest on the roof. Akka, who had been sleeping there, woke up with a start when the lady owl returned. The owl informed her that Flammea, the steeple owl, had granted her request, and had sent her the thing she had wanted.

Since the gray rats had filled the castle rooms without so much as a scratch, they at last felt at ease. Now they took for granted that either all of the black rats had gone to Kullaberg or those who remained had fled, not intending to offer any resistance.

But the gray rats had hardly swallowed the first grains of wheat before they heard the sound of a shrill pipe from the yard. The rats raised their heads, listened uneasily, and ran a few steps as if they had a mind to leave the bins. When the sound died down, they began to eat once more.

Again the pipe sounded a sharp, piercing note; and now something wonderful happened. One rat, two rats, and then hundreds of rats left the grain, jumped from the bins and hurried down to get out of the castle. Not all of the gray rats left, though. They thought of the great value of their conquest of Glimminge Castle, of the delicious grain; and they did not want to leave it. But again they caught the tones from the pipe and had to follow them. With wild excitement they rushed up from the bins, slid down through the narrow holes in the walls, and tumbled over one another in their eagerness to get out.

A tiny creature stood in the courtyard. He was blowing on a pipe, and all around him he had a circle of rats. The rats were astonished and fascinated. More and more rats came to listen.

Once the piper paused, only for a second; he put his thumb to his nose and wiggled his fingers at the gray rats. They pounced at him, to bite him to death; but as soon as he blew on his pipe, they were in his power again.

When the tiny piper had played all the gray rats out of Glimminge Castle, he began to wander slowly from the courtyard out onto the road; and all the gray rats followed him. The tones from his pipe sounded so sweet to their ears that they could not resist them.

The mysterious little creature walked on, charming them as they followed him on the road to Vallby. He led them along turns and bends in the road, through hedges and down into ditches. Wherever he went, they had to follow him.

The pipe he blew on appeared to be made from an animal's horn, although the horn was so small that it must have been broken from the forehead of an animal from a different time, long since forgotten.

No one knew, either, who had made the pipe. Flammea, the steeple owl, had found it in a niche, in Lund Cathedral. She had shown it to Bataki, the raven; and they had decided that this was the kind of horn that was once used to gain power over rats and mice. The raven was Akka's friend, and he had told her that Flammea owned this treasure.

It's true. The rats could not resist the pipe. The boy who was playing it led them as long as the starlight lasted, and then he played at daybreak. The whole time the entire procession of gray rats followed him, enticed farther and farther away from the big grain loft at Glimminge Castle.

THE TRAVELS OF
BOOK ONE
NILS HOLGERSSON

Chapter Five

The Great Crane Dance on Kullaberg

Tuesday, March twenty-ninth.

Although there are many magnificent buildings in Skåne, not a one of them has as pretty walls as old Kullaberg Mountain has.

Kullaberg is low and rather long. No, it's not an imposing mountain. On its broad summit you'll find woods and grain fields, and sometimes a tract of open land covered with small, pinkish-purple flowers. Here and there, you'll see round heather knolls and barren cliffs. Most of the mountain is much like all the other upland places in Skåne.

If you walked along the path that crosses the middle of the mountain, you couldn't help feeling a little disappointed. But if you, perhaps, turned away from the path, wandered off toward the side of the mountain, and looked down over the bluffs, you might see something you didn't expect.

Kullaberg does not have plains and valleys around it, like

other mountains. No, it plunges far out into the sea. Not even the smallest strip of land lies below the mountain to protect it from the mighty waves, which break into foam on the mountain walls, polishing and molding them to suit themselves.

You'll find steep ravines deeply chiselled in the mountain-side and black crags that have become smooth and shiny under the constant lashing of the wind. Solitary columns of rock spring up out of the water, and dark grottoes entice you to explore their narrow entrances, if only you could reach them.

There are barren, perpendicular precipices, and soft, leaf-clad inclines. There are majestic cliff arches projecting over the water. There are small points, small inlets, and small rolling stones that are rattlingly washed up and down with every dashing breaker. Sharp stones are constantly being sprayed by white foam, and other stones are mirrored in unchangeable, dark-green, still water. There are giant troll caverns shaped in the rock and crevices that lure the wanderer to venture into the very depths of the mountain, all the way to Kullman's Hollow.

And over and around these cliffs and rocks crawl entangled weeds. Trees grow there, too, but the harsh winds force the trees to cling like vines onto the steep precipices. The oaks creep along on the ground, and their foliage hangs over them like a low ceiling. Long-limbed beeches stand in the ravines like great leaf tents.

These remarkable mountain walls, with the blue sea beneath them and the clear penetrating air above them, make Kullaberg attractive to people near and far. Crowds of them clamber over the place every day as long as the summer lasts.

What makes Kullaberg so attractive to animals is not known. They assemble there every year. This is a custom that has been observed since time immemorial. To understand why, one should have been there when the first sea wave was dashed into foam against the shore.

To avoid being seen by humans, the stags and roe bucks, hares and foxes, and all the other four-footers make their way to Kullaberg the night before the meeting. Just before sunrise they march up to the playground (a heather heath on the left side of the road, not very far from the mountain's most extreme point). The playground is enclosed on all sides by round knolls, which conceal it.

In the month of May, tourists are not at all likely to stray off up there. By the time of the fall storms, the strangers have been driven away by the cold, unpleasant weather. And the lighthouse keeper out there on the point and the mountain peasant and his family tend to their accustomed routines; they wouldn't bother to go out onto the desolate heather fields.

When the four-footers arrive on the playground, they take their places on the round knolls. Each animal family keeps to itself, although it is understood that, on a day like this, universal peace reigns. No one will be attacked. On this day a rabbit might wander over to the foxes' hill without losing as much as one of his long ears. But still the animals arrange themselves into separate groups. This is an old custom.

After they have all taken their places, they begin to look around for the birds. Strangely, this time they don't see any birds. Why, the sun is high in the sky and they should be on their way!

What the animals do see is a cloud...then another one...and another. And look! One of these clouds is moving along the coast of Öresund, up toward Kullaberg. When the cloud is just over the playground, it stops. Simultaneously, the cloud rings and chips, as if it were made of nothing but shrill tones. At last the cloud falls down over a knoll—all at once—and the next instant the knoll is covered with gray larks, pretty red-white-and-gray bullfinches, speckled starlings and greenish-yellow titmice.

Soon after that, another cloud comes over the plain. This stops over every bit of land; over cottages and palaces; over towns and cities; over farms and railway stations; over fishing hamlets and sugar refineries. Every time it stops, it draws to itself a little whirling column of gray dust; so the cloud grows and grows. And at last, when it heads for Kullaberg, it is no longer a cloud but a whole mist, which is so big that it throws a shadow on the ground all the way from Höganäs to Mölle.

When the mist comes over the playground, the animals can

see it. But gray sparrows rain down on one of the knolls for a long time before the little sparrows in the center of the mist again catch a glimpse of the daylight.

Now the biggest of these bird clouds appears. Formed of birds who have traveled from every direction, the cloud is bluish-gray; and not a ray of sun can penetrate it. It is full of the ghastliest noises, the most frightful shrieks, the grimmest laughter, and most bad-luck-boding croaking! All on the playground are glad when it finally resolves itself into a storm of fluttering and croaking—of crows and jackdaws and rooks and ravens.

Then not only clouds are seen in the heavens, but a variety of stripes and figures. Straight, dotted lines appear in the east and northeast. These are forest birds from Göinge districts—black grouse and wood grouse. They are flying in long lines a couple of yards apart.

Swimming birds that live around Måkläppen, just outside of Falsterbo, now come floating over Öresund in many extraordinary figures—in triangular and long curves, in sharp hooks and semicircles.

Akka and her flock come late, and no wonder. They have had to fly over the entire area of Skåne to get to Kullaberg. Besides, as soon as she awoke, Akka had to go out and hunt for Thumbietot, who had played piper to the gray rats, luring them far away from Glimminge Castle. Mr. Owl had returned with the news that the black rats would be home immediately after sunrise; and since there was no longer any danger, the gray rats could be freed to go where they pleased.

But it was not Akka who located the boy and his long line of followers. Herr Ermenrich, the stork, did! He quickly sank down over Nils, caught him with the bill and swung into the air with him. You see, Herr Ermenrich had also gone out to look for him; and after he had carried him to the stork nest, he asked his forgiveness for rudely tossing him in the air the night before.

This pleased Nils immensely, and the stork and he became good friends. Akka, too, showed him that she was proud of him; she stroked her old head against his arms and commended him for helping those who were in trouble. One thing must be said to

Nils' credit: he did not want to accept praise that he had not earned.

"No, Mother Akka," he said, "I didn't lure the gray rats away to help the black ones. I only wanted to show Herr Ermenrich what I could do."

He had hardly said this when Akka turned to the stork and asked if he thought it was advisable to take Thumbietot along to Kullaberg.

"I believe that we can rely on him as we do upon ourselves," she explained.

"Certainly you shall take Thumbietot to Kullaberg, Mother Akka," Herr Ermenrich said. "We are fortunate to have this means of repaying him for what he endured last night for our sakes. And since it still bothers me that I did not treat him well at first, I will take him on my back, all the way to the playground."

There's nothing better than praise from those who are wise and capable, and the boy had never felt as happy as he did when the wild goose and the stork talked about him this way. And so he made the trip to Kullaberg, riding storkback.

Although he knew that this was a great honor, he was disturbed by Herr Ermenrich's flying. The stork was a powerful flier, and he started off at a very different pace from the wild geese. While Akka flew her straight way with even wing strokes, the stork amused himself by performing flying tricks. Now he lay high in the heavens, without moving a wing muscle; now he shot downward so fast that Nils thought the two of them would be splattered on the ground; now he teased Akka, flying around her in large and small circles, like a whirlwind. And though he clung to Herr Ermenrich in terror, Nils had to admit that until now he had never realized what a strong flier could do.

Only one pause was made during the journey, and that was at Vomb Lake when Akka joined her traveling companions and called to them that the gray rats had been defeated at Glimminge Castle. After that, the travelers flew directly to Kullaberg.

There they descended to the knoll reserved for the wild

geese; and as the boy looked from knoll to knoll, he saw on one the many-pointed antlers of the stags and on another the gray herons' neck crests. One knoll was red with foxes; one was gray with rats; one was covered with black ravens who shrieked continually; and another knoll was spread with larks who simply couldn't keep still, but threw themselves into the air, singing for very joy.

Just as always, the crows began the day's games and frolics with their flying dance. They divided into two flocks that flew toward each other, met, turned, and began all over again. This dance had many repetitions; and to the uninitiated, the dance became monotonous. The crows were proud of their dance, but the other animals were glad when it was over; it seemed as gloomy and meaningless as the winter storm's play with the snowflakes. They waited eagerly for something that offered a little lighthearted pleasure.

They did not have to wait long, either; as soon as the crows had finished, the hares came running. They dashed forward in a long row, without any apparent order. In some of the dance movements, one rabbit ran alone; in others, the rabbits ran three and four side-by-side. They ran so fast, up on their hind legs, that their long ears flopped up and down in all directions. And as they ran, they spun around, jumped high and beat their forepaws against their hind-paws so that they rattled. Some performed a long succession of somersaults. Others doubled up and rolled over like wheels. One stood on one leg and swung around. One walked on his forepaws.

Their antics were humorous, but it was more than humor that made the spectators breathe faster. Now it was spring; summer was coming, and life would be easier. They could all play!

When the hares had romped themselves out, the great forest birds took their turn in the spotlight. Hundreds of wood grouse in shining dark-brown array, and with bright-red eyebrows, flung themselves up into a great oak that stood in the center of the playground. The one who sat upon the branch at the very top fluffed up his feathers, lowered his wings, and lifted his tail so that the white covert feathers were seen. Then he stretched his neck and chirped in deep notes, "Tjack, tjack, tjack!" When he could "Tjack!" no more, he gurgled a few times, then closed his eyes and whispered, "Sis, sis, sis. Hear how pretty! Sis, sis, sis." As he sang, the wood grouse fell into such an ecstasy that he no longer knew what was going on around him.

While he was sissing, the three nearest grouse under him began to sing; and before they had finished their song, the ten who sat lower down joined in the round; and so it continued from branch to branch, until the entire hundred grouse sang and gurgled and sissed. They all fell into the same ecstasy during their song, and this affected the other animals as though it were conta-

gious. Lately the blood had flowed lightly and agreeably; now it began to grow heavy and hot. "Yes, this is spring!" thought all the animal folk. "Winter chill has vanished. The fires of spring are awakening the earth."

When the black grouse saw that the brown grouse were having such success with the audience, they could no longer keep quiet. Since there was no tree for them to fill, they rushed down on the playground, where the heather stood so high that only their beautiful tail feathers and thick bills were visible; and they began to sing: "Orr, orr, orr."

Suddenly, something unprecedented happened. While the animals' attention was on the grouse competition, a fox stole slowly, cautiously, to the wild geese's knoll. He glided way up on the knoll before anyone noticed him. When a goose caught sight of him, she could not believe that a fox had sneaked in for any good purpose.

She cried, "Have a care, wild geese! Have a care!"

The fox struck her across the throat—mostly, perhaps, because he wanted to make her quiet—but the wild geese had already heard the cry, and they rose into the air. All the animals saw Smirre Fox standing on the wild geese's knoll, with a dead goose in his jaws.

Because he had broken the play day's peace agreement, such a punishment was dealt to Smirre Fox that, for the rest of his days, he would regret that he could not control his thirst for revenge. He was surrounded by a crowd of foxes, who judged him in accordance with an old custom. Not a fox wanted to lighten the sentence; they all knew that the instant they attempted anything of the sort, they would be driven from the playground and would never be allowed to play in it again.

Banishment was pronounced upon Smirre without opposition. He was forbidden to remain in Skåne. He was banished from wife and family; from hunting grounds, home, resting places and retreats, which he had owned; and he must try his fortune in foreign lands. In order for every fox in Skåne to know that Smirre was outlawed, the oldest fox bit off his right earlap. Then the young foxes began to yowl from bloodthirst, and they jumped at him. He had no alternative but to run; and with all the young foxes in pursuit, he raced away from Kullaberg.

All this happened while the black grouse and brown grouse were going on with their games. The grouse lose themselves so completely in their song that they neither hear nor see, so they hadn't been disturbed.

Before the forest birds' contest was over, the stags from Häckeberga came forward to show their wrestling game. Several pairs of stags fought at the same time. They rushed at each other with such force that their antlers became entangled. Then they tried to push each other backward. The heath was torn up by their hooves, breath came like smoke from their nostrils, hideous bellowings strained from their mouths, and froth oozed down their shoulders.

On the knolls round about there was breathless silence while the skilled opponents wrestled. New emotions arose in the watchers. They felt courageous, strengthened by returning powers, excited and ready for all kinds of adventures. They felt no enmity toward one another although, if the stags had continued much longer, a wild struggle would have arisen on the knolls. Wings were lifted, neck feathers raised and claws sharpened. All had been gripped by a burning desire to show that they, too, were full of life. Winter's impotence was over, and the power of summer surged through their bodies. But the stags stopped wrestling.

Instantly a whisper went from knoll to knoll: "The cranes are coming!"

They were majestic—these gray, dusk-clad birds with plumes in their wings, and red feather ornaments on their necks! The big birds with their tall legs, their slender throats, their small heads, came gliding down the knoll with a mysterious abandon. They swung around—half flying, half dancing. With wings gracefully lifted, they moved with an inconceivable speed.

There was something marvelous and strange about their dance...as though gray shadows played a game too complex for eyes to follow...as though they had learned it from the mists that hover over desolate morasses. There was witchcraft in it.

Those who had never been on the Kullaberg playground until now understood why the whole meeting took its name from the cranes' dance. There was wildness in it; yet the feeling which it awakened was a wonderful longing. No one thought anymore about struggling. Instead, both the winged and those who had no wings, all wanted to rise eternally, reach above the clouds, seek that which was beyond them, leave the oppressive body that dragged them down to earth and soar away toward the infinite.

Such longing after the unattainable, after the hidden mysteries back of this life, the animals felt only once a year; and this was on the day when they saw the great crane dance.

Chapter Six

In Rainy Weather

Wednesday, March thirtieth.

It was the first rainy day of the trip. As long as the wild geese had remained in the vicinity of Vomb Lake, they had had beautiful weather; but on the day they set out for the north, the weather changed. For several hours the boy had to sit on the goose's back, soaking wet and shivering in the rain.

In the morning, the sky had been clear. The wild geese had flown high up in the air, evenly and without haste. Akka was at the head, maintaining strict discipline, and the rest followed in two oblique lines behind her. They had not taken time to shout witty sarcasms to the animals on the ground, but it was simply impossible for them to be quiet. In rhythm with the wing strokes, they sang out their usual coaxing call: "Where are you? Here I am. Where are you? Here I am."

They only stopped their call occasionally to show the goosey-gander the landmarks they were passing. The places on this route included Linderödsosen's dry hills, Ovesholm's manor, Christianstad's church steeple, Bäckaskog's royal castle on the narrow isthmus between Oppmann's Lake and Ivö's Lake, and Ryss Mountain's steep precipice.

As far as the boy was concerned, this was a monotonous

trip—that is, at least until the rain clouds developed. In the old days, when he had only seen rain clouds from below, he had imagined that they were gray and disagreeable. How different it was to be among them! Now he saw that they were enormous carts which drove through the heavens with sky-high loads. Some of them were piled up with huge, gray sacks, and some with barrels; some were so large that they could hold a whole lake; and a few were filled with huge utensils and bottles. When so many of the cloud carts had been driven forward that they filled the whole sky, someone must have given a signal. All at once, water poured down from utensils, barrels, bottles and sacks.

As the first spring showers pattered on the ground, such shouts of joy arose from the small birds in the groves and pastures that the whole air rang with them.

"Now we'll have rain. Rain gives us spring. Spring gives us flowers and green leaves. Green leaves and flowers give us worms and insects. Worms and insects give us food; and plentiful and good food is the best thing there is," sang the birds.

The wild geese, too, were glad of the rain which came to awaken the growing things from their sound sleep and to drive holes in the ice roofs on the lakes. In spite of their discipline, they were unable to refrain from making merry calls over the neighborhood.

When they flew over the potato patches, so plentiful in the country around Christianstad but still lying bare and black, they screamed: "Wake up and be useful! Here comes something that will awaken you. You have been lazy long enough."

When they saw people hurrying to get out of the rain, they called out, "Why are you in such a hurry? Can't you see that the sky is raining loaves of rye bread and cookies?"

The storm quickly moved northward, close behind the geese. They seemed to think that they dragged the rain clouds with them; and when they saw great orchards beneath them, they announced proudly: "Here we come with anemones; here we come with roses; here we come with apple blossoms and cherry buds; here we come with peas and beans and turnips and cabbages. Whoever wants to can take them. Whoever wants to can take them."

But toward the end of the afternoon, the wild geese grew impatient with the rain. They called out to the thirsty forests around Ivös Lake: "Haven't you had enough? Haven't you had enough?"

The heavens were growing grayer and grayer, and the sun hid itself so well that Nils couldn't imagine where it was. The rain fell faster and faster, and beat harder and harder against the wings as it tried to find its way through the oily outside feathers to their skins. The earth was hidden by fogs. Lakes, mountains, and woods floated together in an indistinct maze; the landmarks could no longer be distinguished. The flight became slower, the joyful cries dwindled into silence at last, and the boy shivered in the cold.

He had been confident as long as he had ridden through the air. And even in the afternoon, when they had landed under a little stunted pine, in the middle of a large bog... Even in the wet, in the cold—where some knolls were covered with snow and others rose naked in puddles of half-melted ice water... Even then he had not felt discouraged. He ran around, feeling quite happy, and hunted for cranberries and frozen whortleberries.

Then evening came. Darkness sank down on him until the wilderness became strangely grim. Even though he was tucked under the goosey-gander's wing, the boy was too wet and cold to sleep. In the darkness, he heard sounds that made him tremble—rustling, stealthy steps, menacing voices.

"Oh, I've got to get away from here!" he thought. "Somewhere with light and heat. What if I went where there are human beings, just for the night? Only so I could sit by a fire and get some food. I could return to the wild geese before sunrise."

Without disturbing the goosey-gander or any of the other geese, he slipped to the ground and stole unobserved through the marsh. He didn't know exactly where he was—if he was in Skåne, in Småland, or in Blekinge. But that evening, when the geese were landing in the bog, he had glimpsed a large village.

That village was his goal. It wasn't long, either, before he found a road; and soon he was on the village street, which was bordered with planted trees and gardens. The boy had come to

one of the big cathedral towns on the uplands.

The houses were of wood, and most of them had gables and fronts that were edged with carved moldings. They had glass doors, with here and there a colored pane, opening on verandas. The walls were painted in light oil colors; the doors and window frames shone in blues and greens, and even in reds.

While Nils walked around and looked at the warm cottages, he could hear the people in them chattering and laughing. Out in the road, he could not distinguish what they were saying, but he thought it was awfully good to hear human voices again.

"What would they say if I knocked and asked to be let in?" he wondered.

This was what he had intended to do all along, but he was no longer afraid of the darkness. The lighted windows had dispelled that fear. Now he was simply shy.

"I'll take a look around the town for a while longer," he thought, "before I ask anyone to take me in."

On one house there was a balcony; and just as the boy walked by, the doors were thrown open and a yellow light streamed through the sheer curtains. A pretty young lady came out on the balcony and leaned over the railing.

"Why, it's raining. Spring will soon be here," she said.

When the boy saw her, he felt a strange anxiety; it was as though he wanted to cry. For the first time he felt uneasy because he had divorced himself from humankind.

After that he walked by a shop. He stopped to look at the red corn planter outside it. Finally he crawled up onto the driver's seat and pretended he was driving the machine over a field. For a moment he forgot that he was a tomten; when he remembered, he quickly jumped down. Now he was distressed; after all, human beings were clever, and they could do a great many things that not even a tomten could do.

He walked by the post office, and then he thought of the daily newspapers, with news from all over the world. He saw the pharmacist's shop and the doctor's home, and he thought about the ability of human beings to battle with sickness and death. When he saw the church, he thought about the people who built it and attended meetings there so they could hear about another world than the one in which they lived—of God and the resurrection and eternal life. And the longer he walked in that town, the better he liked human beings.

Well, it's so. Children rarely think any farther than the length of their noses. Whatever is closest to them holds their attention; they want it immediately, without caring what their desire may cost. A short time ago Nils Holgersson had not understood what he was about to lose when he chose to remain a tomten, but now he began to fear that perhaps he would never regain his humanity.

How could he become a human again? He wanted, oh so much, to know! Crawling up on a doorstep, he sat in the pouring rain and meditated. He sat there one whole hour, then two whole hours. He wrinkled his forehead in thought, but it didn't seem to help; he was none the wiser. Thoughts only rolled around and around in his head. The longer he sat and thought, the more impossible it seemed to find a solution.

"I haven't learned enough to know what to do," he thought at last. "Maybe I'll have to go to a minister and a doctor and a schoolteacher. One of them ought to know of a cure!"

He got up at once and shook himself, because he was as soaked to the skin as a dog that's been swimming in the lake.

Just then a big owl came flying along and alighted on one of the trees bordering the village street. A lady owl, who sat under the cornice of the house, called to him: "Kivitt, kivitt! Are you at home again, Mr. Gray Owl? What kind of a time did you have abroad?"

"Thank you, Lady Brown Owl, I had a very good time," the gray owl replied. "Has anything out of the ordinary happened while I was away?"

(Since Nils was a tomten, he could hear and understand their conversation even though he was several feet away.)

"Not here in Blekinge, Mr. Gray Owl; but a strange thing happened in Skåne! A boy was changed into a tomten, and since then he has been on his way to Lapland with a tame goose."

"That's a remarkable bit of news, a remarkable bit of news.

Can he ever become a human again, Lady Brown Owl? Can he ever become a human again?"

"It's a secret, Mr. Gray Owl. I'll tell you anyway. The tomten said that if the boy watches over the goosey-gander so that he returns home safe and sound..."

"What's that? What's that? Is there another condition, Lady Brown Owl? Another? Another?"

"Fly with me up to the church tower, Mr. Gray Owl, and I will tell you the whole story! I fear that someone may be listening."

With that the owls flew their way. But the boy threw his cap in the air and shouted: "If I watch the goosey-gander so he gets back safe and sound, I will become a human being again! I will become a human being again! I will become a human being again!"

He shouted so long and so loudly that it was strange that no one heard him, but no one did. He hurried back to the wild geese, out in the wet and cold bog, as fast as his legs could carry him.

THE TRAVELS OF
BOOK ONE
NILS HOLGERSSON

Chapter Seven

The Stairway With Three Steps

Thursday, March thirty-first.

The following day the wild geese intended to travel northward through the Allbo district, in Småland. They sent Iksi and Kaksi ahead to find out whether spring had reached that far yet; but when they returned, the scouts said no, all the water was frozen and the land was snow-covered.

The troupe whispered to one another, "We might as well stay where we are. How can we travel over a country where there is neither water nor food?"

"If we remain here, we may have to wait here until the next moon," Akka said, addressing them all. "We had better go eastward, through Blekinge, and see if we can't get to Småland by way of Möre, which lies near the coast and has an early spring."

And so the boy rode over Blekinge the next day. He was in a good mood, now that the night was over and he was warm and dry again. He certainly did not want to give up the trip to Lapland.

"What could have come over me last night?" he wondered. The question in his mind vanished as he looked around from his perch high in the sky.

A thick fog lay over Blekinge so the boy couldn't see what kind of country he was riding over. He tried to search his memory for any information that he might have gotten from his schoolteachers. That, of course, was useless. He knew well enough that he had never been in the habit of studying his lessons.

At once he had a picture in his mind of something he had actually learned in school.

"What?" he thought. "Am I remembering this because I'm a tomten or because I'm still partly a boy?"

The children sat by the little desks and raised their hands; the teacher sat in the lectern and looked displeased; and he himself stood in front of the map and was supposed to answer some question about Blekinge, but he hadn't a word to say. The teacher's face grew darker and darker for every second that passed, and the boy thought the teacher was more interested in geography than in anything else. The teacher came down from the lectern, took the pointer from the boy, and sent him back to his seat.

"What's going to happen now?" The student speculated, a bit worried about the outcome. But the teacher walked over to the window and stood there, looking out. He whistled once, and then he returned to the lectern. He had something to tell them about Blekinge, he said. What he had to say then was so interesting that Nils actually had listened.

"Småland," the teacher said, "is a tall house with spruce trees on the roof, and leading up to it is a broad stairway with three big steps; and this stairway is called Blekinge. The stairway is well-constructed. It stretches forty-two miles along the frontage of Småland house. Anyone who would like to go all the way down to the East Sea, by way of the stairs, has twenty-four miles to walk.

"Years have gone by since the steps of that stairway were hewn from gray stones and laid down, evenly and smoothly, for a convenient track between Småland and the East Sea.

"Since the stairway is so old, one can, of course, understand that it couldn't look the same now as it did way back then, when it was new. No matter how much effort anyone might have exerted, no broom could have kept it clean. After a couple of years, moss and lichen began to grow on it. In the autumn dry leaves and grasses blew over it; and in the spring, it was piled up with falling stones and gravel. All these things were left there to mold, and eventually so much soil gathered on the steps that even bushes and trees could take root there.

"Now the steps look different from one another. The top step, which lies nearest Småland, is covered with poor soil and small stones. The only trees that have survived there in spite of the low temperatures and poor soil are the birches, birdcherries and spruce. The cultivated fields, ploughed up from the forest lands, are tiny; the cabins and people who live in them are few in number; and there are great distances between the churches.

"There is better soil on the middle step; and it is not bound by the low winter temperatures, either. The trees are higher and of finer quality. You'll find maple, oak, linden, weeping birch and hazel trees, but no cone trees to speak of. The cultivated fields are larger, the people have great and beautiful houses, and there are many churches with large towns around them. In every way the middle step looks better than the top one.

"But the lowest step is the best of all. It is covered with good rich soil; and where it bathes in the sea, it hasn't the slightest Småland chill. Beeches, chestnut and walnut trees thrive down there, and they grow so big that they tower above the church roofs. Here, too, are the largest grain fields. The people benefit not only from farming, but from fishing, trading and seafaring. For this reason you'll find the grandest residences and most impressive church structures here; and the parishes have developed into villages and cities.

"But that is not all there is to be said about the three steps. When it rains on the roof of the big Småland house, or when the snow melts up there, the water has to go somewhere. Then, naturally, a lot of it spills over the big stairway. In the beginning it probably flowed over the whole stairway, big as it was; and then

cracks appeared in it. Now the water flows alongside the stairway in dug-out grooves.

"And water is water. It cannot rest on a slope. In one place it cuts and files away, and in another it deposits sediment. The grooves it has dug into vales. The walls of the vales it has decked with soil, and bushes and trees and vines have clung to them ever since—so thick and in such profusion that they almost hide the stream of water that winds its way down there in the deep. But when the water reaches the landings between the steps, it's thrown headlong in such a seething rush that it gathers enough strength to move mill wheels and machinery (these, too, have sprung up by every waterfall).

"There is still more to be said of the land with the three steps. Up in the big house in Småland, a giant once lived. He had grown old, and no longer cared to have to walk down that long stairway in order to catch salmon from the sea. To him it seemed a better idea for the salmon to come up to him.

"So he climbed up the roof of his house and began to throw boulders over the whole of Blekinge and down into the East Sea. When the boulders crashed down, the salmon were so scared that they fled from the sea into the Blekinge streams, through the rapids and over the waterfalls to the feet of the old giant.

"You'd know this is true if you could see the number of islands and points that lie along the coast of Blekinge; they're the boulders that the giant threw. The salmon also prove that this story is true, because they always go up the Blekinge streams, working their way up through rapids and still water, all the way to Småland.

"The Blekinge people should feel grateful for the ingenuity of that old giant, because the salmon in the streams and the stonecutting on the island have created industries that provide a living for many of them."

THE TRAVELS OF
BOOK ONE
NILS HOLGERSSON

Chapter Eight

By Ronneby River

Friday, April first.

Neither the wild geese nor Smirre Fox had believed they would ever meet again after they left Skåne. But it turned out that the wild geese happened to take the route over Blekinge, and that was where Smirre Fox had gone.

So far he had remained in the northern parts of the province; and since he hadn't discovered any manor parks or hunting grounds stocked with game and young deer, he was as disgruntled as he could be.

One afternoon when Smirre was tramping around in the desolate forest district of Mellanbygden, not far from Ronneby River, he saw a flock of wild geese; and one of them was white!

"Aha! I'll cause them some trouble now!" he thought to himself, and he began to hunt the geese. He did it just as much for the pleasure of getting a good meal as for the desire to be avenged for the humiliation they had heaped on him.

He saw that they were headed east, toward Ronneby River. Then they changed their course and followed the river south. He realized that they intended to find a roost for the night along the riverbanks.

"Getting one or two geese for my supper should be easy," he

thought. He was hungry! But when he located the place where they had taken refuge, he saw that it was well protected and he couldn't get near.

Ronneby River is a little river, as rivers go; but it is well-known for its scenic beauty. At several points it forces its way between steep mountain walls that jut out of the water, and are overgrown with honeysuckle and bird cherry, mountain ash and osier.

But the cold and blustery spring-winter weather kept the wild geese and Smirre Fox from thinking how beautiful the river might be in a few weeks. The geese were glad that they had found a large strip of sand at the foot of a steep and impassable mountain wall. Overhanging branches screened them. As they settled down for the night, they watched the river in front of them; it rushed past, violent and strong in the snow-melting time.

Night came, and all the geese were asleep. But the boy was awake. Fear of darkness and the wildness of the wilderness had overwhelmed him again. Where he lay—tucked in under Morton Goosey-Gander's wing—he couldn't see anything, and he could only hear a little.

"What if something happens to the goosey-gander? What will happen to me then? He won't be able to save me."

Nils heard noises and rustlings from every direction, and he grew so uneasy that he had to creep from under the wing and look around. But he stayed close to the gander.

Longsighted Smirre leaned over the precipice and glared at the wild geese below him. He was cranky.

"I might as well forget supper. I can't climb down this mountain wall to get a goose. I can't swim in such a wild river, and there isn't a single strip of land below the mountain that leads to their roost."

But Smirre, like all foxes, found it hard to admit defeat—even to himself. So he lay down at the very edge of the precipice and watched the wild geese. While he watched, he thought of the harm they had done him. Yes, it was their fault that he had been driven from Skåne and was forced to move to poverty-stricken Blekinge. As he thought, he grew angrier and angrier.

"I wish they were dead, even if I couldn't eat a single one of them!"

When Smirre was beside himself with rage, he heard rasping in a large pine near him. A squirrel was running for its life, hotly pursued by a marten. Neither animal noticed Smirre; and he sat quietly and watched the chase, which went from tree to tree.

He looked at the squirrel, who moved among the branches as lightly as though he could fly. He looked at the marten, who was not as skilled in climbing as the squirrel, but who still ran up and along the branches just as securely as if they had been forest paths.

"If only I could climb as well as either of them," Smirre wished, "those geese down there wouldn't sleep in peace for long!"

As soon as the squirrel had been captured and the chase was over, Smirre padded over to the marten. He stopped two steps away from him to signify that he would not cheat him of his prey. Smirre greeted the marten in a friendly manner and complimented him on his catch. Smirre chose his words well, as foxes do.

The marten, on the contrary, hardly answered him. Although with his long and slender body, his fine head, his soft skin, and his light-brown neck fur, the marten was a marvel of beauty, he was in reality a crude forest dweller without any conception of politeness whatsoever.

"It surprises me," Smirre said, "that such a fine hunter as you are would be satisfied with chasing squirrels when there is much better game within reach."

Here Smirre paused; but when he saw that the marten was grinning impudently at him, he continued.

"Haven't you seen the wild geese at the foot of this mountain wall? But maybe you aren't a good enough climber to get down to them."

This time he didn't need to wait for an answer. The marten jumped at him with back bent and every hair on end.

"Have you seen wild geese?" he hissed. "Where are they? Tell me instantly, or I'll bite your neck off!"

"Oho, you'd better be careful. Remember, my little friend, that I am twice your size. So be a little polite. I'm more than happy to show you the wild geese."

Within a minute the marten was on his way down the steep wall. While Smirre watched him swing his snakelike body from branch to branch, he thought: "That pretty tree hunter has one of the most wicked hearts in all the forest. The wild geese will have me to thank for a bloody awakening."

Suddenly the marten was tumbling down from branch to branch, and he landed—plop!—in the river. Wings beat loudly, and all the geese flew into the air.

Smirre was amazed. What had happened? He sat waiting until the marten came clambering up. The poor thing was soaked in mud, and stopped every now and then to rub his head with his forepaws.

"I might have known you'd botch up the hunt," Smirre said contemptuously.

"You don't need to scold me," the marten said. "I sat on one of the lowest branches, thinking how I would tear the geese to shreds. All at once a little creature, no bigger than a squirrel, jumped up and threw a rock at me. It knocked me into the river, and..."

The marten didn't have to say more; he no longer had an audience. Smirre was already in pursuit of the wild geese.

In the meantime, Akka had flown south in search of

another roost. The half-moon was high in the heavens, so the lead goose could still see a little. She was well-acquainted with this part of the country, because she had been wind-driven to Blekinge before, when she flew over the East Sea in the spring.

She followed the black, snaking river all the way to Djupafors. At Djupafors the river hides in an underground channel, then rushes down through a narrow cleft and breaks against the bottom in glittering drops and flying foam. Below the falls lie a few boulders among which the water rushes away in a furious torrent. Akka made a difficult landing on one of the slippery boulders.

This was another good roost, especially this late in the evening, when no human beings were around. At sunset the geese would not have been able to camp here, because Djupafors is far too close to people. On one side of the falls is a paper factory; on the other is Djupadal's Park, where people climb around on steep paths to enjoy the stream's swift current.

The wild geese never gave a moment's thought to the famous park. To them, the place was dangerous; they had to stand and sleep on wet stones in the middle of a rumbling waterfall. At least they were safe from their predators.

They fell asleep, and again Nils stood guard. He remembered quite clearly that the condition for his becoming a human being again was to take good care of the white goosey-gander.

After awhile, Smirre Fox came running along the shore. He saw the geese standing among the foaming whirlpools, and he knew that he couldn't get at them there, either. Sitting on the shore, he just looked at them. He felt that his reputation as a hunter was at stake.

Then he noticed an otter creeping up from the falls with a fish in his mouth. Smirre approached him. As with the marten, he stopped within two steps of the otter to show him that he wouldn't attempt to steal his game.

"Mr. Otter, you are very modest. Why, you're content with catching a fish when the boulders in the river are covered with geese!"

The otter ignored the fox. He didn't even turn his head in the direction of the river. He was a vagabond, like all otters, and he knew Smirre Fox.

"I know how you act when you want to coax away a salmon trout," he snorted.

"Oh! Is it you, Gripe?" said Smirre.

He was delighted, because he knew that this particular otter was a quick and accomplished swimmer.

"I'm not surprised that you won't even look at the wild geese. Why, you couldn't manage to get out to them if you wanted to."

But the otter (who had swimming webs between his toes, a stiff tail for an oar, and waterproof skin) didn't want anyone to think that there was a waterfall he couldn't manage. He turned to look at the river; and as soon as he caught sight of the wild geese, he dropped the fish and rushed down the shore into the river.

If it had been a little later in the spring, so the nightingales had been there, they would have sung a rhapsody of Gripe's perilous struggle with the rapids. The otter was thrust back by the waves many times, and carried downstream; but he fought his way up again and again. Finally he reached the geese.

Smirre followed Gripe's course as well as he could in the dim moonlight, and at last he saw the otter climb up to the wild geese. Then the otter shrieked and fell back into the water. He rushed away in the rapids like a drowning kitten. An instant later, there was a great crackling of geese's wings. Akka and her flock flew off to find another sleeping place.

Gripe eventually crawled back on shore. Without saying a word, he began to lick one of his forepaws. When Smirre sneered at him because he hadn't succeeded, he retorted: "It was not the fault of my swimming art, Smirre. I was about to pounce on a goose when a tiny creature came running and jabbed me in the foot with some sharp iron. It hurt so that I lost my footing, and then the current took me." He needn't have explained. Smirre was already far away in pursuit of the wild geese.

Once again Akka and her famous entourage had to make a night flight. Fortunately, the moon had not yet gone down; and with the aid of its light, she followed the shining river south. Over Djupadal's manor and over Ronneby's dark roofs and white waterfalls she swayed forward without alighting. But a little south of the city and not far from the sea, she flew toward the Ronneby health spring, with its bathhouse and springhouse; with its big hotel and summer cottages for the spring's guests. All these stand empty in winter, which the birds know perfectly well; and many companies of birds seek shelter on the deserted buildings' balustrades and balconies during storms.

Akka landed on a balcony; and as usual, the geese fell asleep at once. Since the boy could not sleep after his adventures, he sat there and saw how pretty it looked where sea and land meet, here in Blekinge.

You see the sea and land can meet in different ways. In many places the land approaches the sea with flat, tufted meadows; and the sea meets the land with flying sand, which piles up in mounds and drifts. One would think the land and sea disliked each other so much that they offered only the poorest they owned.

It can also happen that where the land leans toward the sea, it raises a wall of hills in front of it, as though the sea were dangerous. Where the land does this, the sea pushes against it in wrath, roaring and lashing against the rock, and looking as if it would tear the land to pieces.

In Blekinge it is altogether different where land and sea meet. There the land breaks up into points and islands and inlets, and the sea divides into fjords and bays and sounds. And it is this, perhaps, which makes it look as though the land and sea meet in happiness and harmony.

Think about the sea. Far out it lies desolate and big, and it has nothing to do but roll its gray billows. When it advances toward the land, it crosses the first obstacle. This it immediately overpowers—tears away everything green and makes it as gray as itself. Then the sea meets another obstacle. With this it does the same thing. And still another. Yes, the same thing happens to this one. It is stripped and plundered.

Then the obstacles come closer and closer together, and a strange thing happens. The sea realizes that the land is sending her littlest children ahead of her to offer peace and friendship. Then the sea is moved to pity. It also becomes more friendly the farther in it comes—rolls its waves less high, moderates its storms, lets the green things stay in cracks and crevices, separates into small sounds and inlets, and becomes at last so harmless that little boats dare venture out on it. Why, the sea cannot recognize itself—so mild and friendly it has grown.

And then think of the hillside. It lies uniform and looks the same almost everywhere. It consists of flat grain fields with an occasional birch grove, or else of long stretches of forest ranges. Apparently the hillside is entirely concerned with grain and turnips and potatoes and spruce and pine. Then a sea fjord cuts far into it. The hillside doesn't mind that, but borders it with birch and alder, as if it were an ordinary freshwater lake. Then still another wave drives in. The hillside borders it just like the first one.

Then the fjords begin to broaden and separate, breaking up fields and woods. The hillside cannot but notice them then!

"I believe it is the sea itself that is coming," says the hillside, and then it begins to adorn itself. It wreathes itself with blossoms, travels up and down in hills and throws islands into the sea. It no longer cares about pines and spruce, but casts them off like old, everyday clothes, and parades later with big oaks and lindens and chestnuts, and with blossoming leafy bowers, and becomes as gorgeous as a manor park. And when it meets the sea, the hillside is so changed that it doesn't know itself.

All this one cannot see very well until summertime. At any rate, the boy observed how mild and friendly nature was, and he began to feel better. Just when he was about to climb back under the goosey-gander's wing, he heard a sharp and ugly yowl from the bathhouse park. Nils looked over the balcony and saw a fox standing on the pavement below.

Smirre had followed the flock once more. But when he found their quarters and realized that he couldn't get at them, he yowled in chagrin. He was disappointed and humiliated and vexed. Oh!

The sorry-looking fox awakened Akka, and she recognized the voice.

"Is that you, Smirre?"

"Yes, it is I," he said, thinking fast. "And I want to ask what you geese think of the night that I have given you."

"Do you mean to say that you sent the marten and otter against us?" asked Akka.

"A good turn shouldn't be denied," he said. "You once

played the goose game with me, and now I have begun to play the fox game with you. I won't let up on it as long as a single one of you remains alive, even if I have to follow you around the world!"

The goose answered, "You, Smirre, ought to be ashamed of yourself. Why should you, weaponed with teeth and claws, hound us so? We are defenseless!"

Smirre thought he sensed fear in the old goose's words, and he spoke quickly: "Akka, if you throw Thumbietot down to me, I'll make peace with you and never pursue you or any of yours again."

"I'm not going to give you Thumbietot," said Akka. "From the youngest of us to the oldest, we would willingly give our lives for his sake."

"Since you're so fond of him, then," said Smirre, "I promise you now that he will be the first among you to taste my vengeance!"

Akka said no more, and after Smirre tired of yowling, all was still. The boy lay awake. Now it was Akka's words that kept him from sleeping. He had never dreamed that anyone would risk life for his sake. From that moment, it could not be said of Nils Holgersson that he did not care for anyone.

THE TRAVELS OF
BOOK ONE
NILS HOLGERSSON

Chapter Nine

Karlskrona

Saturday, April second.

It was a moonlit evening in Karlskrona, calm and beautiful. But earlier in the day, there had been wind and rain; and people were not yet venturing out on the streets.

While the city lay so quiet, Akka and her flock of wild geese came flying toward it over Vemmön and Pantarholmen. They were out in the late evening to find a roost on the islands. They could not remain inland because wherever they landed, Smirre Fox was there to disturb them.

While the boy was riding along, high up in the air, contemplating the sea and islands below, he thought uneasily that the whole scene had begun to look spooky. The heavens were no longer blue, but like green glass. The sea was milk-white; and small, silver-tipped waves rolled as far as he could see. In the midst of all this white lie a myriad of islets, absolutely coal black. Whether they were big or little, whether they were as flat as meadows or full of cliffs, they looked just as black. Even houses and churches and windmills, which at other times were white or red, were outlined in black against the green sky. The boy thought it was as if he had come upon another world.

Nils wanted to be brave, but he saw something up ahead that frightened him. It was a high cliff island covered with big, angular blocks; and bright, golden flecks—like fireflies—shone among the blocks. He wondered if the shining flecks were anything like the Maglestone, by Trolle-Ljungby, that trolls sometimes mounted on high pillars.

And horrid things were lying all around the island. Maybe they were whales and sharks and other sea monsters; or maybe they were sea trolls who had gathered around the island and intended to crawl up on it and fight with the land trolls who lived there. Nils thought that those on the land were probably afraid, too, because he saw a big giant with upraised arms as if in utter despair. He saw it right there, on the highest point of the island.

At that very moment, Akka began to cruise downward, right over the island.

"No, Akka! Not there!" the boy cried. "We must not land there!"

But the wild geese continued to descend, and soon Nils had a better look at the place. Why, the big stone blocks were nothing but houses. The whole island was a city, and the shining gold specks were street lamps and lighted window panes. The giant, who stood highest up on the island and raised his arms, was a church with two cross towers. All the sea monsters and trolls, which he thought he had seen, were boats and ships that lay anchored around the island. Mostly rowboats, sailboats and small coast steamers were anchored on the side which lay toward the land. Grand battleships were on the side that faced the sea.

"Battleships!" Nils exclaimed. "This must be the magnificent city of Karlskrona that Grandpa told me about."

All his life he had been interested in ships, although he'd only seen them in his imagination—that is, except for the miniature galleys he had sailed in the road ditches back home.

The boy's grandfather had once been a Marine; and as long as he had lived, he had talked about Karlskrona every day—of the great warship dock and of all the other things to be seen in that city. The boy felt perfectly at home, and he was to actually see what his grandfather could only tell him about.

But Nils got only a glimpse of the towers and fortifications barring the entrance to the harbor, and the buildings, and the shipyard, before Akka descended to one of the flat church towers.

"Well, this should be a safe place for anyone who hopes to get away from a fox!" Nils thought to himself, and he decided to get a little sleep under the goosey-gander's wing. Perhaps he

would try to see more of the dock and ships in the morning.

He certainly had not slept five minutes before his curiosity got the best of him. He slipped out from under the wing and slid down the church tower's lightning rod, then down the waterspout all the way down to the ground.

Soon he stood on a big square in front of the church. It was covered with round stones, and was just as difficult for him to travel over as for big people to walk on a tufted meadow.

Those who live way out in the country feel on edge when they enter a city—where the houses stand straight and forbidding, and the streets are open so that everyone can see who's there. Nils felt that way. When he stood on Karlskrona Square and looked at the German church, and the town hall, and the cathedral from which he had just climbed, he wished that he was back on the tower with the geese.

It was a lucky thing that the square was deserted. There wasn't a human being about, unless he counted a statue representing a big, brawny man in a three-cornered hat, long waistcoat and knee breeches. Nils couldn't tell who the statue man was supposed to be, but he held a walking stick; and he looked as though he knew how to use it, too. He had an awfully mean expression on his face, with a big, hooked nose and an ugly mouth.

"What is that long-lipped thing doing here?" the boy wondered, with a shiver.

He had never felt so small and insignificant as he did then. He tried to bolster his nerve by saying something flippant to the statue. Then he forgot about it and turned down a wide street leading to the sea.

Someone was following him. He sensed it. Someone was

walking behind him, who stamped on the stone pavement with heavy footsteps and a hard stick. It sounded as if the bronze man in the square had gotten down from the pedestal and gone for a walk.

Nils began to run. He still heard the footsteps behind him, and he was more convinced than ever that the bronze man was behind him. The ground trembled, and the houses shook; and the boy became panic-stricken when he thought of the impudent comments he had made to him.

"Maybe he's just out for a stroll and... Could he really have been that upset about what I said? Statues don't walk! Oh-h-h-h... This one does!"

The boy quickly turned east into a side street. He had to get away from the bronze man!

But the statue switched off to the same street; and his steps were ever so much bigger than the boy's, and how hard it was to find any hiding places in a city where all the gates were closed! Nils was running for his life. Then he saw on his right an old frame church, which lay a short distance from the street, in the center of a large grove.

"If only I can get to the church, then I'll be shielded from harm!"

As he ran toward the church, he caught sight of a man who beckoned to him.

"There's someone who will help me!" thought the boy, and he hurried off in that direction.

But when he reached the man, who stood on the edge of a gravel path, he was astonished.

"No! It couldn't be! Was the man who beckoned to me made of wood?"

Nils stood there and stared at him. The carved statue was of a thickset man on short legs, with a broad, reddish face. He had shiny, black hair and a full, black beard. He had a wooden hat; on his body, a brown wooden coat; around his waist, a black wooden belt. On his legs, he had wide wooden knee breeches and wooden socks; and on his feet, black wooden shoes. He was newly painted and varnished, so that he glistened in the moonlight.

In his left hand there was a wooden slate, and there the boy read:

Most humbly I beg you,
Though voice I may lack:
Come drop a penny, do;
But lift my hat!

Why, the man was only a poor-box. Nils felt like a fool. And now he remembered that his grandfather had mentioned the wooden man and that all the children of Karlskrona were fond of him. That must have been true, too, because Nils found it hard to part with the wooden man. He had something so old-timey about him that one could well take him to be many hundred years old; and at the same time, he looked so strong and bold—and animated, it's true—just as one might imagine people looked hundreds of years ago.

For awhile there, Nils had forgotten about the bronze man. But now he heard him again. The statue was in the churchyard. He'd followed him even here! Suddenly, the wooden man bent down to the tiny boy and stretched out his broad, wooden hand. With one jump, the boy was in his hand. The wooden man lifted him to his hat, and stuck him under it.

In a second, Nils' pursuer was there, almost before the wooden man could get his arm in the right place again. The bronze man banged his cane on the ground, so that the wooden man shook on his pedestal.

"Who might this one be?" the bronze man demanded.

The wooden man's arm went up, creaking in the old woodwork; and he touched his hat brim as he replied: "Rosenbom, by Your Majesty's leave. Once upon a time boatswain on the man-of-war Dristigheten; after completed service, sexton at the Admiral's church; and lately, carved in wood and exhibited in the churchyard as a poor-box."

The boy gave a start when he heard the wooden man say "Your Majesty." For now, when he thought about it, he realized that the statue on the square represented the one who had founded the city. It was probably no less than Charles the Eleventh himself.

"He gives a good account of himself," said the bronze king. "Can he also tell me if he has seen a little brat running loose in the city tonight? The uncivil child! If I get my hands on him, I'll teach him manners!"

He again pounded the ground with his cane, and his scowl was enough to scare almost anyone.

"By Your Majesty's leave, I have seen him," said the wooden man; and the boy shook with fear. He peeked at the bronze king through a crack in the wooden man's hat. When the wooden man said, "Your Majesty is on the wrong track," Nils began to feel better.

"The boy must've been heading for the shipyard, where he could find a hiding place."

"Well, then, Rosenbom, come and help me catch him. Get down from that pedestal! Four eyes are better than two, Rosenbom."

But the wooden man answered in a sad voice: "I would most humbly beg to be permitted to stay where I am. I look well and sleek because of the paint, but I'm old and moldy, and cannot stand moving about."

The bronze king was not one of those who liked to be contradicted.

"What sort of notion is this? Come along, Rosenbom!"

He raised his walking stick and whacked the wooden man on the shoulder.

"Does Rosenbom see that he holds together?"

"Yes, Your Majesty."

With that, the wooden man stepped down from his pedestal and followed the bronze king. They walked through the streets of Karlskrona until they came to a high gate, which led to the shipyard. Just outside the gate and on guard walked one of the Swedish Navy's jack-tars (sailors), but the bronze man strutted past him and kicked the gate open without the jack-tar's noticing it.

As soon as they were in the shipyard, they saw the wide harbor separated by pile bridges. Battleships were moored in the harbor basins, and they looked bigger and even more impressive than they did when Nils saw them from the sky.

"Where does Rosenbom think it most advisable for us to look?" asked the bronze king.

"Such a small boy would probably try to conceal himself in the museum hall of models," replied the wooden man.

Many old buildings were crowded on the narrow strip of land, which stretched to the right from the gate and all along the harbor. The bronze man walked directly to a low building with small windows. He pounded on the door with his walking stick until it burst open, and tramped up a pair of worn-out steps. With his little friend still under his cap, the wooden man followed the king inside.

Soon they were in a large hall, which was filled with miniature, full-rigged ships. These were models of the ships that had been built for the Swedish Navy—ships of many kinds. There were old men-of-war, with sides bristling with cannons and masts weighed down with sails and ropes. There were small island boats with rowing benches along the sides. And there were cannon sloops and richly gilded frigates, which were models of the ones the kings had used on their travels. Finally, there were heavy, armor-plated ships with towers and cannons on deck (such as were used in Nils' day); and narrow, shining torpedo boats that resembled long, slender fish. Nils was awed.

"Think of it! These great ships have all been built in Sweden!"

Nils had plenty of time to see all that was to be seen in the museum; when the bronze king saw the models, he forgot everything else. He examined them all, from the first to the last, and asked about them. Rosenbom, formerly boatswain on the Dristigheten (in charge of rigging, anchors, cables, and such), told as much as he knew of the ships' builders and of those who had manned them. He told the king about Chapman and Puke and Trolle, of Hoagland and Svensksund. The boatswain's recitation ended with the year 1809; he hadn't been there after that. Both he and King Charles the Eleventh had the most to say about the fine, old, wooden ships.

"I can hear that Rosenbom doesn't know anything about the new-fangled battleships," said the bronze king. "We shall go and look at something else. This tour amuses me, Rosenbom."

The king had forgotten about the boy, who felt secure where he sat under Rosenbom's wooden hat. Both the bronze king and the wooden poor-box man wandered through the shipyard. They peered through the windows of the sail-making shops, the anchor smithy, machine and carpenter shops. They saw the mast sheers and the docks, the large magazines, the arsenal, and the rope bridge. They walked past a big, discarded dock. The two old seadogs went out on the pile bridges, where the naval vessels were moored, stepped on board and examined them—wondered, disapproved, approved, and became indignant.

Nils heard everything they said about the people who had worked in the shipyard—how they had struggled to equip the navies that had gone out from here. He heard how life and blood had been risked, how the last penny had been sacrificed to build the battleships, how skilled men had strained themselves to perfect the ships that had been their fatherland's safeguard. More than once, tears came to the boy's eyes as he listened.

The two tour guides (as Nils would call them) then went into an open court, where the galley models of old men-of-war were grouped. Nils gasped when he saw them. The men-of-war seemed big, fearless and savage—filled with the proud spirit of the sailors who manned them. They were from another time. Nils felt very humble.

"Take off thy hat, Rosenbom, for those that stand here!" the bronze king said. "They have all fought for the fatherland."

And Rosenbom, like the bronze King Charles the Eleventh, had forgotten why they had made this tour. Without thinking, he lifted the wooden hat from his head and shouted:

"I take off my hat to the one who chose the harbor and founded the shipyard and recreated the navy; to the monarch who has awakened all this into life!"

"Thanks, Rosenbom! That was well spoken. Rosenbom is a fine man. But what is this, Rosenbom?"

There stood Nils Holgersson, right on the top of Rosenbom's bald pate. Nils wasn't afraid any longer, but raised his white toboggan hood and shouted: "Hurrah for you, Longlip!"

The bronze king struck the ground hard with his walking stick, but the boy never found out what he had intended to do. The sun had just come up over the horizon, and the two statues had vanished with its first rays.

While he was standing there in the courtyard, the wild geese flew up from the church tower and swayed back and forth over the city. When they caught sight of the boy, the big white goose darted down from the sky and swung him onto his back. On they went to new adventures!

THE TRAVELS OF
BOOK ONE
NILS HOLGERSSON

Chapter Ten

The Trip to Öland

Sunday, April third.

The wild geese went out to a wooded island to feed. There they happened to run across a few gray geese, who were surprised to see them. Their kinsmen, the wild geese, usually travel far inland.

The gray geese were curious, and they wouldn't be satisfied until they had heard all about the persecution Akka and her flock had suffered from Smirre Fox. When the tale was told, a gray goose, who appeared to be as old and as wise as Akka herself, said: "It was a great misfortune for you that Smirre Fox was declared an outlaw in his own land. He'll be sure to keep his word and follow you all the way to Lapland.

"If I were in your place, I would not travel north over Småland. I would take the outside route over Öland instead, so that Smirre will be thrown off the track. To really confuse him, you should remain on Öland's southern point for at least two days. There you will find food and plenty of company. That's my suggestion."

Akka agreed—yes, that was sensible advice; and she decided to take it. As soon as the wild geese had eaten all they could hold, they started on the trip to Öland. None of them had ever been there before, but the gray goose had given them excellent directions. They only had to travel directly south until they came to a large bird track, which extended all along the Blekinge coast. All the birds who had winter residences by the West Sea, and who now intended to travel to Finland and Russia, followed that bird track. And, they were always in the habit of stopping at Öland to rest. The wild geese would have no trouble finding a guide.

That day it was perfectly still and warm—the best kind of day for a sea trip. The only problem was that it was not quite clear. The sky was gray, and enormous clouds hung way down to the sea's outer edge, obstructing the view.

Far out from the wooded island, the sea became as glassy-smooth as a mirror. Looking down from his seat on the goosey-gander, Nils thought the sea had disappeared. The water had reflected the sky so perfectly that it had become one with the sky.

All of a sudden, Nils was dizzy. There was no earth beneath him. Only mist and sky were around him. He held onto the goose's back as if he were about to fall in any direction. What was up and what was down, what was east and what was west, he had no way of knowing.

The boy felt even worse when the wild geese reached the bird track. Flock after flock came flying in exactly the same direction. They seemed to follow a fixed route. There were ducks and gray geese, surf-scoters and guillemots, loons and pintail ducks and mergansers and grebes and oyster catchers and sea-grouse.

But now, when the boy leaned forward and looked for the sea, all he could make out was the sea's reflection of the whole bird procession.

"Are the birds all flying upside down?" he wondered, feeling a little sick.

Nils was so confused that he didn't know what to do with himself. And the geese were tired and impatient. They were not in the least inclined to joke or tease, or even to make their usual coaxing call. Everything seemed unreal to the boy.

"What if we have left earth behind and are traveling to heaven?" he speculated.

Just about then he heard loud shots and saw two white columns of smoke. Nils' dizziness passed all at once.

The birds cried: "Hunters! Hunters! Fly high! Fly away!"

Then Nils knew, finally, that the wild geese had been traveling over the seacoast; and they certainly weren't ready to fly to heaven. A long row of hunters in rowboats were firing shot after shot into the air. The flocks of birds that had come upon them first hadn't noticed them in time. They had flown too low. Several dark bodies sank toward the sea; and for every one that fell, cries of anguish arose from the living.

It was strange for someone who had only a moment before believed that he was on the way to heaven, to wake up to such fear and sorrow. Akka shot upward as fast as she could, and the flock followed. The wild geese (including Morton Goosey-Gander and his tiny companion) got safely out of the way.

Considering hunting from this new perspective, Nils couldn't help but think, "How could anyone wish to shoot such as Akka and Yksi and Kaksi and the goosey-gander and the others! Human beings have no conception of what they do."

The birds continued on their way. Everything was as quiet as before, with the exception that some of the tired birds called out every now and then: "Are we almost there? Are we on the right track?"

Those who flew in the center answered: "We are flying

straight to Öland, straight to Öland."

The gray geese could barely fly anymore, and the loons passed them.

"Loons! Loons! Don't be in such a rush!" the ducks called reprovingly. "You'll eat up all the food before we get there."

"Oh, there'll be enough for both you and us," the loons answered.

Before they had gotten close enough to see the outline of Öland on the horizon, a light wind came up, pushing against them. It brought with it something like immense clouds of white smoke, as if there were a fire somewhere. When the birds saw the first spiral haze, they became uneasy and increased their speed. The clouds grew thicker and thicker, at last enveloping them altogether.

They were in a dense fog! When it became so thick that one couldn't see a goose-length ahead, the birds began to carry on like lunatics. If they had flown in perfect order before, now they flew hither and thither, trying to entice one another astray.

"Be careful!" they cried. "You're only flying round and round. Turn back! You'll never get to Öland this way."

They all knew where the island was; but there were rogues in the group, and they were determined to get there first. In the fog, they could create utter confusion!

"They are going back toward the North Sea!"

"Take care, wild geese!" shrieked someone from another direction. "If you continue like this, you'll get all the way up to Rügen."

The birds who were accustomed to this route could not be lured in a wrong direction, but the wild geese had a rough time.

"Where do you propose to go, good people?" called a swan. He came right up to Akka, and looked sympathetic and serious.

"We want to reach Öland, but we haven't been there before," Akka said. She thought that this was a bird to be trusted.

"That's too bad," replied the swan. "You're going in the wrong direction. You're on the way to Blekinge. Follow me. I'll show you the way."

And so he flew off with them; and when he had taken them so far from the bird track that they could no longer hear the calls, he disappeared in the fog. They had been tricked!

They flew around for awhile at random. They had barely succeeded in finding the birds again, when a cocky duck approached them.

"You'd better settle down on the water until the fog clears," he said. "It's evident that you are not accustomed to look out for yourselves on journeys."

Akka could have done without the duck's comment, but she didn't say a word.

"Be careful! Can't you see that you're flying upside down?" shouted a loon as he rushed by.

Upside down! The boy positively clutched the goosey-gander around the neck. This was something he had feared for a long time.

No one knows when the geese would have arrived if they hadn't heard a muffled, rolling sound in the distance. Akka craned her neck, snapped hard with her wings, and sped on. The gray goose had told her not to land on Öland's southern point, because there was a cannon there. (The people used it to shoot the fog.) Now Akka knew her way, and no one could lead her astray again.

THE TRAVELS OF
BOOK ONE
NILS HOLGERSSON

Chapter Eleven

Öland's Southern Point

April third to sixth.

On the southern side of Öland, there lies a royal domain called Ottenby. This large estate extends from shore to shore, straight across the island; and it is remarkable because it has always been a haven for birds. In the seventeenth century, when the kings went to Öland to hunt, the estate was a deer park. In the eighteenth century, there were stables for breeding thoroughbred racehorses and a sheep farm, where several hundred sheep were maintained. In Nils' time, there were neither racehorses nor sheep at Ottenby. Instead, there were herds of young horses, which were to be used by the Swedish cavalry.

In all of Sweden there is no better place for animals. Along the eastern shore lies the old sheep meadow, which is one and one-half miles long and the largest meadow in all of Öland, where animals can graze and play, as free as if they were in a wilderness. Here you will find the renowned Ottenby grove with the hundred-year-old oaks, which provide shade from the hot sun and shelter from the strong Öland winds. And we must not forget the long Ottenby wall, which separates Ottenby from the rest of the island.

You will find plenty of tame animals at Ottenby, but that

isn't all. The wild ones also feel sheltered and protected on the old crown property. Besides, there are still a few stags of the old descent left; and burrow-ducks and partridges live there. The swampy eastern shore offers a resting place for thousands of migratory birds in the spring and late summer.

When the wild geese and Nils Holgersson had finally found their way to Öland, they came down, like all the rest, on the shore near the sheep meadow. The fog lay thick over the island, just as it had over the sea. But the boy was amazed to see all of the birds on the narrow stretch of shoreline that was within his tomten vision.

It was a sandy beach with stones and pools and cast-up seaweed. If the boy had been given a choice, he probably wouldn't have thought of landing there; but the birds looked upon this as a veritable paradise. Ducks and geese fed on the meadow. Snipe and other birds ran nearer the water. Loons paddled in the sea and fished. Other birds were busy picking grubworms on the seaweed banks along the coast.

The great majority planned to travel farther and had only stopped to take a short rest. When one leader of a flock thought that his comrades had recovered sufficiently he said, "If you are ready now, we may as well move on."

"No, wait, wait! We haven't had nearly enough."

"Oh, come now. Do you really think I'll let you eat until you can't get off the ground?"

He flapped his wings and started off, and his flock reluctantly followed.

A flock of swans rocked on the gentle waves in the shoals. Now and then they dove down and brought up food from the sea floor. When they'd gotten something especially good, they trumpeted their pleasure.

Nils was anxious to see the swans, since he had never seen any at close range. He hurried out to the seaweed banks to look at the majestic birds.

The boy was not the only one who had heard the swans trumpet. The wild geese and the gray geese and the loons swam out. They bobbed among the waves, in a circle around the swans.

The regal white birds ruffled their feathers, raised their wings like sails, and lifted their beautiful necks in the air. Occasionally one of them swam up to a goose, or a great loon, or a diving duck, and said a few gracious words. And then it appeared as though the one addressed hardly dared raise his bill to reply.

But there was a young loon—a tiny, mischievous snippet—who couldn't stand all this ceremony. He dived, disappearing under the water. Soon after, one of the swans screamed and swam off so quickly that the water foamed. One after another of the swans screamed in surprise.

The little loon wasn't able to stay under any longer, but popped back up on the water's surface. The swans rushed toward him; but when they saw the little bird, they turned abruptly. They wouldn't bother to quarrel with a mere fledgling.

Then the little loon dived again. He pinched their feet. That must have hurt; and the worst of it was, the swans couldn't maintain their dignity. They beat the air with their wings until it thundered; went forward a ways, as if running on the water; caught sufficient wind under their wings, and flew into the air. Their audience was sad to see them go, and they scolded the little loon for his thoughtless antics.

The boy walked toward land again. There he watched the

pool-snipe playing. They resembled small storks; they had a little body, long legs and neck, and light, swaying movements. Only they were not gray, but brown. They stood in a long row on the shore where it was washed by waves. As soon as a wave rolled in, the whole row ran backward; as soon as it receded, they followed it. And they kept this up for hours.

The showiest of all the birds were the burrow-ducks. They were undoubtedly related to the ordinary ducks. Like them, they had a thick body, broad bill, and webbed feet. But, they were much more elaborate. The feather dress, itself, was white. But around their necks they wore a broad gold band; the wings shone in green, red, and black; and the head was dark green, and it shimmered like satin.

When a few burrow-ducks happened on shore, one of the other birds remarked: "My, look at that! They certainly know how to dress."

"If burrow-ducks were less conspicuous, they wouldn't have to burrow in the ground to make their nest; they could lay their eggs above ground like anyone else," a brown mallard said.

"Oh, I don't think they're so attractive," a gray goose apparently couldn't keep from saying. "They'll never get anywhere with a nose like that." And it's true. The burrow-ducks had a big knob on the base of the bill, which did nothing to enhance their appearance.

Close to shore, seagulls and sea swallows were fishing.

"What kind of fish are you catching?" asked a wild goose.

"Stickleback. It's Öland stickleback. It's the best stickleback in the world," said a gull. "Would you like to taste it?"

The gull flew over to the goose, with his beak full of the little fish, and offered her some. She recoiled, shaking her head.

" No! I wouldn't touch it!"

The next morning, the sky was just as cloudy. The wild geese fed on the meadow, and the boy went off to gather mussels. There were plenty of them on the seashore, and he decided to take some along on the trip. He found an old sedge plant; and he braided its tough, woody stems into a knapsack for the mussels.

When it was time for the main meal of the day, the wild geese came running and asked Nils if he had seen anything of the white goosey-gander.

"No, he hasn't been with me," the boy said.

"He's been with us until just lately," Akka said, "but now we don't know where he is."

The boy jumped up, terribly frightened. He asked if any of the geese had seen a fox or eagle around, or if a human being had been in the neighborhood. But no one had noticed anything dangerous. The goosey-gander had probably lost his way in the fog.

But nothing they could say would satisfy Nils. He ran off to hunt for Morton Goosey-Gander. The fog shielded him so that he could run without being seen, but it also prevented him from seeing well. He ran south along the shore—all the way down to the lighthouse and the fog cannon on the island's extreme point. But no goosey-gander was to be found there. Nils ventured over to the Ottenby estate; and he searched every one of the old, hollow oaks in Ottenby grove. He saw no trace of the bird.

He searched until sundown, and then he had to turn back again to the eastern shore. He walked slowly and sadly. He didn't know what would become of him if he couldn't find the goosey-gander.

But as he was wandering over the sheep meadow, what did he see but Morton Goosey-Gander. The bird was all right, but very glad that Nils had found him. The fog had made him so dizzy, he said, that he'd lost his way. Nils threw his arms around the big bird's neck and asked him to be careful and not to wander away from the others. No, never again, said the bird.

But the next morning, when the boy went down to the beach and hunted for mussels, the geese came running and asked if he had seen the goosey-gander. No, of course he hadn't.

"Well, then, the goosey-gander's gotten himself lost again."

Frightened, the boy ran off to search again. He found a place where the Ottenby wall was so broken down that he could climb over it. Later he looked on the shore, which gradually widened so there was room for fields and meadows and farms. Then he looked up on the flat highland, in the middle of the island, where the only buildings to be seen were windmills and where the turf was so thin that the white limestone shone through it. But when evening came, he still hadn't found his friend.

Nils was climbing back over the Ottenby wall when he heard a stone fall close to him. As he turned to look, he thought he could distinguish something moving. He crept nearer and saw the goosey-gander trudging wearily over a pile of stones, with something in its bill. The goosey-gander didn't see the boy, and the boy did not call to him. Instead, he watched him.

Nils soon learned why Morton Goosey-Gander was there by the wall. A young gray goose lay among the stones, and she cried with joy when she saw the goosey-gander. Nils stole closer, so he could hear what they said. Then he found out that one of the gray goose's wings was wounded so that she could not fly. Unable to help her, her flock had left her behind.

She had been near death when the white goosey-gander heard her call the other day and had found her. They had both hoped that she would be well before they left the island, but she still could neither fly nor walk. At last the gander said good-night and promised to return the next day.

As soon as he was gone, Nils climbed up the stone heap to the goose. He was angry because he had been deceived, and he wanted the gray goose to know that the goosey-gander was his property. He wouldn't hear of the goose's staying here to take care of her.

But when he saw the young gray goose up close, he understood not only why the goosey-gander had gone and carried food to her for two days, but also why he had not wanted to mention that he had helped her. She had the prettiest little head; her feather dress was like soft satin, and the eyes were mild and pleading.

When she saw the boy, she tried to run away; but the left wing was out of joint and dragged on the ground, interfering with her movements.

"Don't be afraid of me," the boy said. "I'm Thumbietot, Morten Goosey-Gander's friend."

Then he stood there. He didn't know what else to say.

Occasionally one meets animals that have a strange aura, as if they were transformed human beings. Nils sensed the magic. The gray goose lowered her neck and head very charmingly before him, and said in a voice so pretty that he couldn't believe it was a goose who spoke: "I am very glad that you have come here to help me. The white goosey-gander has told me that no one is as wise and as good as you."

She expressed herself with such dignity that the boy grew embarrassed.

"She must be a bewitched princess," he thought, with awe.

He wanted—oh, so much!—to help her. With her consent, he ran his hand under the wing feathers and felt along the wing-bone. The bone was not broken, but there was something wrong with the joint. He got his finger down into the empty cavity.

"Hold still, now," he said, and got a firm grip on the bone-pipe and adjusted it correctly. He did it quickly, but it must have hurt. The goose cried out and then sank down among the stones without showing a sign of life.

The boy was terribly frightened. He had only wanted to help her, and now she was dead. He jumped down from the stone pile and ran away. He felt as though he had murdered a human being.

The next morning, the fog had lifted and Akka was ready for the next leg of the journey. All the wild geese were ready to go, but Morton Goosey-Gander made excuses. The boy knew why, but Akka ignored the goosey-gander and started off.

Nils jumped up on his back, and the white one followed the flock, although slowly and unwillingly. The boy was glad that they could fly away from the island. His conscience bothered him because he hadn't told Morton Goosey-Gander what had happened, yet he wondered how the white one had the heart to leave the young gray goose.

Suddenly the goosey-gander turned. The thought of the poor gray goose had overpowered him. He couldn't go with the others when he knew that she was alone and ill, and would starve to death. With a few wing strokes he was over the stone pile; but then, where was the young goose?

"Dunfin! Dunfin! Where are you?" he called.

"The fox has probably been here and taken her," thought the boy.

But a pretty voice answered the goosey-gander: "Here I am, Goosey-Gander! Here I am! I've only been taking a morning bath."

The little gray goose was fresh and trim; and she told Morton Goosey-Gander how Thumbietot had pulled her wing into place, and that she was entirely well and ready to follow them on the journey.

The drops of water lay like pearl dew on her shimmery satin-like feathers, and Thumbietot thought once again that she was a real little princess.

THE TRAVELS OF
BOOK ONE
NILS HOLGERSSON

Chapter Twelve

The Big Butterfly

Wednesday, April sixth.

The geese traveled alongside the coast of Öland Island, flying low enough so that Nils could see what lay beneath them. The boy was just as happy as he had been depressed the day before, when he roamed the island, hunting for the goosey-gander.

He saw now that the interior of the island consisted of a barren high plain with a wreath of fertile land along the coast, and he began to understand something that he had heard the other evening.

He had just sat down to rest by one of the windmills on the highland when two shepherds and their dogs came along, followed by a large herd of sheep. The boy had not been afraid because he was hidden under the windmill stairs. As it turned out, the shepherds sat down on those very stairs.

One of the shepherds was young, and he looked like other people. The other, much older, was a trifle odd. His body was large and worn by the years; but his head was small, and his face had sensitive, delicate features. His body and head just didn't seem to fit each other at all.

The old shepherd sat silently and gazed into the mist, with

an unutterably weary expression. Then he began to talk to his companion. The other one took some bread and cheese from his knapsack, to eat his evening meal. He hardly said a word in response, but he listened very patiently, as if he were thinking: "I might as well give you the pleasure of letting you talk a while."

"I'll tell you something, Erik," the old man said, "I believe that in former days, when human beings and animals were much larger than they are now, the butterflies must have been gigantic. And once upon a time there was a butterfly that was many miles long, and it had wings as wide as seas. The wings were blue and shone like silver. They were so gorgeous that when the butterfly was flying, everyone stood still and stared at it.

"The butterfly had one drawback. It was too large. The wings could hardly carry it. Probably the butterfly would have been all right, though, if only it had been wise enough to remain on the hillside. But it wasn't. It ventured out over the East Sea. And it hadn't gotten very far before a storm arose and tore at its wings.

"Well, Erik, it's easy enough to understand what would happen to those frail butterfly wings. They were torn away and scattered, and the poor butterfly fell into the sea and drowned. At first it was tossed back and forth on the billows, and then it was cast onto a few cliffs outside of Småland. And there it lie.

"Now I think that if the butterfly had dropped on land, it would soon have rotted and fallen apart. But since it fell into the sea, it was soaked through and through with lime, and became as hard as stone. You and I have found stones that looked like petrified worms. I think that the same thing happened to that butterfly body. I believe it turned into a long, narrow mountain out in the East Sea. Don't you?"

He paused for a reply, and the other one nodded to him.

"Go on," he said, without offering his own opinion or a question about the older man's logic.

"And mark you," the old shepherd continued, "this very Öland, upon which you and I live, is the butterfly body. If you think about it, you can observe that the island is a butterfly. Toward the north, the slender, top part of the body and the head can be seen; and toward the south, the lower part of the body, which broadens and then narrows to a point."

Here he paused once more and looked at his companion rather anxiously to see how he would take this hypothesis. But the young man kept on eating and nodded to him to continue.

"Well, as soon as the butterfly had been changed into limestone, many different kinds of seeds of herbs and trees came traveling with the winds, and took root on it. But years passed before anything but tufts of sedge would grow there. Then came sheep sorrel, rock rose, and thorn bush. Even today there isn't much growth on Alvaret. That mountain is covered, sure enough, but it shines through here and there.

"No one can plow or sow up there, you know, because the soil is so shallow. But if you will admit that Alvaret and the rock formations around it are made of the butterfly body, then you just might question where the land that lies beneath those unusual formations came from.

"Yes, the question had crossed my mind."

"You know as well as I do that Öland has existed in the sea for a good many years. Well, in the course of time, all the miscellaneous objects that tumble in the waves—the seaweed and the sand and clams, and so forth—have gathered around Alvaret and remained there. And then, stone and gravel have fallen down from both the eastern and the western rock formations. That's how the island has acquired broad shores, where grain and flowers and trees can grow.

"Up here on the hard butterfly back, the soil is thin. That's why only sheep and cows and horses are kept here. Only lapwings and plover live here, and there are no buildings except windmills and a few stone huts for shepherds. But down on the coast, where the soil is much deeper, there are big villages and churches and parishes and fishing hamlets and a whole city."

He looked questioningly at his companion, who had finished his meal and was tying the lunch sack together.

"How far will you take your line of reasoning?"

"Only this far. This is what I want to know," said the shepherd. He lowered his voice, practically to a whisper; but Nils, who had the uncanny hearing of a tomten, heard every word.

"Do the peasants who live on the built-up farms, or the fishermen who take the small herring from the sea, or the merchants in Borgholm, or the bathing guests who come here every

summer, or the tourists who wander around in Borgholm's old castle ruin, or the sportsmen who come here in the fall to hunt partridges, or the painters who sit here on Alvaret and paint the sheep and windmills... Do any of them understand that this island was once a butterfly?"

"Ah!" the young shepherd replied. "It should have occurred to at least some of them that this island could not have come into existence like the others. They might have thought the same as you—as they sat on the hillside in the evening, and heard the nightingales trill in the groves below them, and looked out over Kalmar Sound."

The old shepherd mused dreamily, "I'd like to know if anyone has ever wanted to build wings on the windmills—wings so large that they could reach to heaven, so large that they could lift the whole island out of the sea and let it fly like a butterfly among butterflies."

"Of course it may be possible that other people have felt that way," said the young one. "On summer nights, when the heavens widen and open over the island, I have sometimes thought that the island wanted to raise itself from the sea and fly away."

But once the old shepherd had gotten the young one to talk, he didn't listen to him very much.

"I would like to know," he dreamed aloud, "if anyone can explain why I feel such a longing up here on Alvaret. I have felt it every day of my life, and I think that everyone who comes here feels that mysterious longing. I wonder if anyone else has come to the conclusion that this wistfulness is caused by the fact that this island is actually a butterfly longing for its wings."

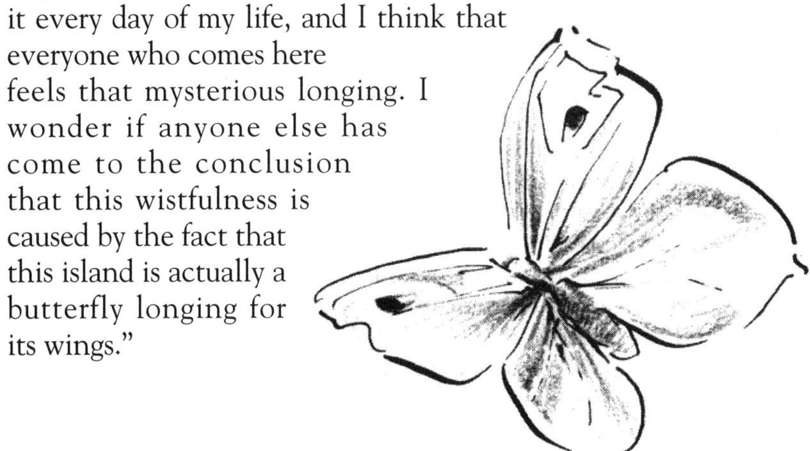

THE TRAVELS OF
BOOK ONE
NILS HOLGERSSON

Chapter Thirteen

Little Karl's Island

The Storm

Friday, April eighth.

After a quiet night on Öland's northern point, the wild geese were on their way to the continent. A strong south wind over Kalmar Sound had blown them toward the north, but they had made good headway.

All at once, as they neared the first islands, they heard a loud rumbling, and the water beneath them turned black. Akka drew in her wings so suddenly that she almost came to a full stop. Then she dived toward the water. Before she and her flock could settle there, the hurricane winds were upon them. Blinded by the fog and pelted by salt scum, the geese were caught with hundreds of small birds, tossed end over end, and thrown far out over the East Sea.

There at least, they could land on the water. Although the sea was whipped by the wind until its green billows surged and rolled higher and higher, with seething foam on their crests, the wild geese were unafraid. They let the waves carry them high on the crests and low in the water dales—going up and down, up and down, like children on playground swings. They were not out of danger, though. The rocking waves made them want to poke their bills under their wings and go to sleep.

Akka called anxiously, "Don't go to sleep! If you fall asleep, you will get lost! Beware! You will get lost! You will get lost!"

No matter how hard they tried not to, one after another fell asleep. Akka herself was about to doze off, when she suddenly saw something round and dark rise on the top of a wave.

"Seals! Seals! Seals!" she screamed and rose up in the air. The alarm came just in time. Before the last wild goose had time to fly up from the water, the seals were so close to her that they made a grab for her feet.

Again the wild geese were swept up by the roaring winds and driven across the desolate sea. Whenever the geese landed on the water, they rocked and slept, only to be awakened just seconds before the seals could catch them. If old Akka had not been alert, not one of her flock would have escaped.

The storm raged all day, causing havoc among the crowds of migrating small birds. Some were driven off course to foreign lands, where they would die of starvation. Others became so exhausted that they fell into the sea and drowned. Many became prey for the seals. At last, Akka wondered if she and her flock would also perish. They were tired, and there was no place to rest.

Toward evening, ice appeared on the sea. In the violent winds, the chunks of ice shifted and crashed together, and Akka refused to land on the water for fear of being crushed. Twice the geese tried to stand on the floating ice. The first time, the winds washed them into the sea. The second time, the seals came creeping up on the ice.

At sundown the wild geese were flying with the last strength they had, afraid of the night to come. Distressed bird cries had sounded over the sea all day long. No one could help; all were struggling to save themselves. Now in the growing darkness, the hopeless cries were terrifying. Down on the sea, the ice flows banged and grated, and the seals sang their wild hunting songs. Heaven and earth, it seemed, were about to clash.

The Sheep

Clutching Morton Goosey-Gander's back feathers, the shivering little tomten stared down at the violent waves. Without warning, the howling wind grew into a savage roar. Nils looked up. The flock was about to crash into a cliff!

Akka had seen the danger in time, however, and steered her charges toward the half-round entrance of a cave. Safe at last, the wild geese immediately counted heads to see if anyone was missing. Akka was there. So were Iksi, Kolmi, Nelja, Viisi, Knusi, all six goslings, the goosey-gander, Dunfin and Thumbietot. Where was Kaksi from Nuolja? No one knew.

"Dear Kaksi, she's old and wise, well able to take care of herself," the geese thought to themselves. "If anyone would know how to find her way back, Kaksi would."

Putting any fears out of their minds, the geese began to explore the cave. Enough light came in through the opening so that they could see that the cave was both deep and wide. They were delighted that Akka had found such a fine night harbor—that is, until one of them caught sight of some shining, green dots, which glittered in a dark corner.

"They're animal eyes!" cried Akka. The geese made a frantic rush for the cave opening.

"Wait!" Thumbietot shouted. "The animals in the corner are sheep. They won't hurt you!"

The geese looked back. When they had accustomed themselves to the dim light in the cave, they could see the sheep. There were adults (about as many as there were in the flock of wild geese) and a few little lambs. An old ram with long, twisted horns appeared to be the most lordly one of the flock. Akka went up to him with much bowing and scraping.

"Well met in the wilderness," she greeted, but the big ram lie still and did not speak a word of welcome.

"Are we not permitted to be here?" asked Akka. "We have been driven by the winds all day. What a relief it would be to stay here tonight!"

Not a word could be heard in response, but some of the

sheep heaved deep sighs. Akka knew that sheep were always shy, but these seemed peculiarly unable to know how to conduct themselves. Finally an old ewe with a sad expression on her face said, "Of course you may stay overnight, but this is a place of mourning and we cannot receive guests as we would under different circumstances."

"You need not serve us; no, not anything of the sort," Akka said. "If you knew what we have endured, you would understand how grateful we are just to rest in safety."

The ewe answered sadly, "It would be better for you to fly in the storm than to stay in this unhappy place, yet none of us would want you to leave before we have had the privilege of offering you our hospitality."

Akka bowed once again, and then she followed the old ewe to a hollow in the ground, which was filled with water. Beside it lie a pile of husks and chaff, and the ewe encouraged Akka and her flock to make the most of this meager fare.

"We have had a hard winter," the ewe explained. "The peasants who own us bring us just enough hay and oat straw to keep us from starving. This is all that is left."

The geese rushed at the food and ate every bit of it. They must have noticed that the sheep were anxious, but the thought of danger did not occur to them.

When the geese began to nod off to sleep, the big ram got up and walked over to them, startling them out of their drowsiness. The animal was not only immense in size, but he had a high, rolling forehead, intelligent eyes and a confident bearing. He looked proud and courageous.

"I cannot assume the responsibility of allowing you to remain without warning you that this place is unsafe. For your own good, you should not plan to stay overnight."

"We will leave, since you really think we should go," Akka said. "But won't you tell us what is wrong? We don't even know where we are."

"This is Little Karl's Island," the ram replied, "just outside of Gottland. Only sheep and seabirds dwell here."

"Are you wild sheep?" Akka asked, hoping that the ram would become more informative.

"You might say we are wild, though not entirely. We have nothing to do with human beings. It's an old agreement between us and some farmers in Gottland that they will supply us with fodder in severe winters; in payment, they are allowed to thin out our flock. The island is small, so it cannot support many of us. Otherwise we take care of ourselves all year round."

"You seem to lead a better life than tame sheep," Akka said. "What could be troubling you?"

The old ram paused as if to decide how much to tell her. Then he said, "The winter was bitterly cold. The sea froze, and three foxes came over. They stayed to plunder us."

"Oh, do foxes dare to attack you?" Akka asked, surprised.

"No, no! not during the day; then I can protect myself and my flock," he replied, shaking his horns. "The foxes sneak up at night when we are asleep. We try to keep awake, but we have to sleep sometime. Because of that, the foxes have slaughtered entire flocks that were once as large as mine."

The ewe broke in, "We hate to admit that we are as helpless as tame sheep."

"Do you think the foxes will come tonight?" Akka asked.

"They were here last night," the ewe said, "and they stole a lamb. They'll come again and again—as long as any of us are alive."

"Why, then you will be exterminated!" Akka exclaimed.

"It won't be long," the ewe agreed.

Akka hesitated before she said anything more. She was unwilling to venture out into the storm again, yet this cave was not the haven of safety that she had expected.

"Thumbietot," she called, "come over here." When the little tomten ran over to her, she said, "Would you be willing to stand guard tonight?"

"Yes, Mother Akka," he said.

"I'm sorry that you won't get any rest after such a hard day," she continued, "but if the foxes attack, you must awaken us in time to fly away."

"Please don't worry," the boy said. "I will stay awake all night." He was glad not to have to go out in the storm again. He walked down to the cave opening and crawled behind a stone that provided him shelter from the wind and still enabled him to watch the entrance.

After awhile, the storm began to abate and the sky cleared. Moonlight played on the waves. Nils climbed outside the cave and looked around. The cave was high up on the cliff, and a narrow path led to it.

So far, he had not seen a fox. Down there on the strip of land below the cliff were what looked like huge trolls. Maybe they were made of stone, maybe they were actually human beings, or maybe they were figments of his imagination. Some had big, thick heads. Others had no heads at all. Some were one-armed. The boy worked himself into a panic, forgetting all about the foxes.

Then he heard a claw scrape against a stone, and he saw three foxes coming up the path toward him. That shook him out of his dream world! At the same time, his courage returned. It struck him that rousing the wild geese would be a pity.

Instead, he ran to the big ram and pulled on his horns until he awoke. Then he swung himself up on the animal's back and urged, "Get up, Ram. Let's frighten the foxes!"

The foxes must've heard the noise. When they reached the cave entrance, they stopped.

"Did you hear what I heard?" one fox asked.

"Oh, go ahead!" another said. "You can't be afraid of sleepy old sheep, can you?"

The three padded quietly into the cave. Then they stopped and sniffed the air.

"Who shall we take tonight?" whispered the boldest fox.

"Let's take the ram. Then we can feast on the others whenever we wish. They won't have the heart to stand up against us."

Nils and his mighty companion had been watching closely. Now the boy shouted, "Butt straight forward!" and the ram hit the first fox—head over tail—back to the opening.

"Butt left!" he shouted, turning the big ram's head in that direction. The ram made a terrific assault on the second fox, who tumbled over and over before he got to his feet and raced for safety. Oh, how Nils wished that the third fox could have gotten some of the same treatment, but he was already gone.

"I think they've had enough for tonight," the boy said with satisfaction.

"Ah yes, I would say so," the ram agreed. "Now lie down on my back and climb under my thick wool. You deserve to be warm and comfortable tonight."

Hell's Hole

The next day the big ram showed Nils around the island. Little Karl's Island was a miniature mountain, and it looked like a large house with perpendicular walls and a flat roof. The roof was the first place the ram took his little tourist. He showed him the good grazing land up there, and Nils had to admit that the island seemed to be especially good for sheep. Even the food—the sheep-sorrel and little spicy growths, still hidden in snow—seemed to have been created for the woolly animals.

Nils looked at the sea, which now lay blue and sunlit, rolling forward in glittering swells. To the east lay Gottland, and to the southwest lay Great Karl's Island, which looked very much like this little island. When the ram took Nils to the very edge of the mountain roof, so the boy could look down, he noticed birds' nests on the steep walls. Surf-scoters, eider ducks, kittiwakes, guillemots and razor bills swam on the sea below. They were so pretty and peaceful, fishing for small herring.

"This is a wonderful place to live," he reflected, "and so pretty!"

"Oh, it's pretty enough here," the old ram said with a nod. He looked as if he might say more, but refrained. "If you explore this island alone, watch out for the crevices that run all around the mountain." It was a good warning because there were deep and broad crevices in many places. The largest was called Hell's Hole and was many fathoms deep and nearly six feet wide.

"If anyone fell down there, he could not survive," the ram said. Nils thought his warning was unnecessarily pointed, but said nothing.

Then the ram conducted the boy down to the narrow strip of shoreline so he could see the giants that had frightened him the night before, at close range. They were nothing but tall pillars of rock. The ram called them cliffs.

Although the shoreline itself was beautiful, Nils was shaken by the ghastly piles of dead sheep. Here was where the foxes had held their orgies. He saw bare skeletons, half-eaten carcasses and others that had been left untasted. Why, the foxes had thrown themselves on the sheep just for sport—just to hunt them and tear them to death.

The big ram walked by the dead in silence, then climbed up the mountain again. He stopped and said meaningfully, "If someone were capable of helping us, and he had seen our misery, how could he rest until the foxes were punished?"

"Well," the boy said hesitantly, "even the foxes have to live."

"True enough," the old ram said. "Those who hunt solely to provide food for themselves and their litters have a right to their sustenance. But these foxes are felons."

"The peasants who own Little Karl's Island should help you," the boy insisted.

"They have rowed over a number of times," the ram replied, "but the foxes hid in the caves and crevices, so the peasants could not get near enough to shoot them."

"You don't think I can help you, do you? A tiny creature like me? When even the peasants and you could not get the better of them?"

"You who are so little can do many things that bigger creatures cannot do," the ram answered.

Neither said any more about this, and the boy went over to the wild geese, who were feeding on the highland. Although he had not cared to show his feelings to the ram, he would have been glad to help the sheep.

"I can at least talk to Akka and Morten Goosey-Gander about what the ram said," Nils said to himself. "Perhaps they can offer a suggestion."

The next day the white goosey-gander took the boy on his back, and the two of them explored the island. The gander wandered around, apparently unconscious of how large and white and delicious he would look to a fox. Why he wasn't more careful was a wonder, because he had fared rather poorly in the storm. He limped on his right leg, and the left wing hung and dragged as if it might be broken. He pecked at a blade of grass here and another there, never once looking around for possible danger.

Nils lay full-length on the goosey-gander's back, looking up at the blue sky. He was so accustomed to riding now that he no longer worried about falling off.

The foxes were watching. Sneaking so cautiously that the goosey-gander couldn't see so much as a shadow of them, they came closer and closer. Then they leaped.

Then the gander must have noticed something, because he ran out of their way, and they missed him. Anyway, the poor thing was limping away as fast as he could.

The boy sat up and faced the foxes, teasing them: "Ha! You can't even catch a goose. You've gotten too fat from eating mutton!"

The foxes lunged, unaware that they were near Hell's Hole. Two yards from the massive crack in the rock, Nils patted Morton Goosey-Gander on the neck and said, "Fly up." The goose rose into the air with one wing stroke.

In an instant they heard wild howls behind them, scraping claws, and heavy falls. The foxes were gone!

The next morning the lighthouse keeper on Great Karl's Island found a bit of bark poked under the door. On it had been cut in slanting, boyish lettering, "The foxes on the little island have fallen into Hell's Hole. Take care of them!"

The lighthouse keeper did, too.

THE TRAVELS OF
BOOK ONE
NILS HOLGERSSON

Chapter Fourteen

Two Cities

The City at the Bottom of the Sea

Saturday, April ninth.

It was a calm and clear night. Since the foxes were gone, the wild geese did not seek shelter in any of the caves on Little Karl's Island. They stood and slept on the flat mountaintop, enjoying the fresh air. The boy had lain down in the short, dry grass beside them.

The moonlight was so bright that night that Nils Thumbietot Holgersson could not sleep. About three weeks had gone by since he had begun his trek with the wild geese. Why, this was Easter-eve! He sat up. This was a special night.

Every year on this night, all the witches come home from Blakulla. He laughed to himself. He was a little afraid of sea nymphs and tomtens, but he didn't believe in witches the least little bit. Well, if any witches had been out, he was sure that he would have seen them. The sky was so bright that not the tiniest speck could move in the air without his seeing it.

While the boy lay there with his nose in the air, he mused on the beautiful moon. The disk was whole and round, high in the night sky. Over it a big bird was flying—not on top of the moon, but across its face. The bird did not pass it, either, but seemed to fly out of it straight toward the boy.

The bird looked black against the light background, and its wings extended from one rim of the disk to the other. He flew on evenly, in the same direction. The body was small, the neck long and slender, and the legs hung down, long and thin; it had to be a stork.

Seconds later, Herr Ermenrich landed beside the boy. The stork bent down and poked him with his bill to awaken him. Instantly the boy sat up.

"I'm not asleep, Herr Ermenrich. Why are you out in the middle of the night? Are the black rats attacking Glimminge Castle again? Do you want to talk to Mother Akka?"

"Don't get excited, my little friend," the stork answered patiently. "I couldn't sleep either, so I decided to hunt you up. The seamew told me you were spending the night here."

Nils was amazed to think that Herr Ermenrich would travel so far and so late at night to talk to him. They chatted about all sorts of things. Then the stork asked him if he would like to go for a ride.

"Oh, yes!"

A ride on the back of this superior flier would be an adventure in itself. After the stork promised to return to the wild geese before sunup, the two set out. Herr Ermenrich flew straight toward the moon. His flight was so light and easy that Nils could have been floating on air. When the stork descended, the boy was disappointed; the ride was far too short for him.

"Look around while I rest, Thumbietot. Don't go so far, though, that you can't find your way back!" Herr Ermenrich stood on a sand hill, drew up one leg and snuggled his bill under his wing.

Well now, why would the stork land here? What a desolate seashore! All Nils could see were sand dunes. When he walked up a sand hill to see how the land behind it looked, he stubbed the toe of his wooden shoe against something hard. He stooped down and saw a small copper coin on the sand. It was practically worthless, so he kicked it out of his way.

When he stood up again, he was puzzled. Something strange had happened to the landscape. Where there had been nothing but sand and a few banks of seaweed, now there was a high, dark wall with a turreted gate. Silently the big gate opened.

"This must be the work of a ghost," Nils thought, but he

couldn't see any dangerous trolls or any other evil around. Oh, the gate was more beautiful than any he had ever seen! What was behind it? He ran inside to look.

Guards sat and threw dice under the magnificent archway leading into the mysterious city. Nils was afraid that they would see him, but they took no notice of the tiny creature. They looked oddly foreign, those men, with their puffy, brocade suits. Why did they remind the boy of something he had seen before?

Beyond the arch, Nils came upon an open square that was paved with large stone blocks. All around the square stood impressive buildings with long, narrow streets between them. The square itself was full of human beings, and they all looked as rich as kings and queens!

Princely men wore long, fur-trimmed capes over satin suits, plumed hats, and superb gold and silver chains. Regal women wore high headdresses and long gowns with tight-fitting sleeves.

"Now I remember," the boy reflected. "I've seen pictures of a place like this—in the old storybook in Mother's chest!"

Every house had an elaborately decorated gable facing the street—so showy, in fact, that Nils wondered if the people who owned the gables had tried to outdo one another. One imposing gable, which stair-stepped from the very top ridgepole of the house down to the eaves, showcased figurines of Christ and the Apostles. Some gables were inlaid with sparkling, multicolored glass; others were striped and checked with white and black marble.

"I'd better hurry," Nils thought suddenly. "Maybe this dreamland will vanish before morning."

He saw people everywhere, and everyone was busy, busy, busy. Old women sat by their open doors and spun without a spinning wheel—only with the help of a shuttle. The merchants' shops were like market stalls, opening on the street. All the

laborers did their work outside. In one place they were boiling crude oil, in another tanning hides. Nils saw armorers hammering out thin breastplates; shoemakers soling soft, red shoes; weavers inserting silver and gold into their weaving.

All around the city was a high fortress wall. The boy saw it at the end of every street. On the top of the wall strode knights in shining armor. When Nils reached the far end of the city, he ran outside the gate that stood there. He saw old ships with rowing benches and high structures fore and aft. Some took on cargo, while others were just casting anchor.

Back into the city he ran, down to the center square. There stood the massive cathedral with its three high towers and deep-vaulted arches sheltering religious images, each one of them an artistic masterpiece. Not a stone of the cathedral was without its own special ornamentation. Gilded crosses, gold-trimmed altars and priests in golden vestments shimmered through the open gate.

Across the street was the courthouse, a building with a notched roof and a slender, sky-high tower. Everything he had seen was wonderful, but Nils was growing tired. He no longer ran in excitement, but leisurely rambled around.

Perhaps people had thought he was a little gray rat darting helter-skelter, but now he could be seen much better. A cloth merchant noticed him and beckoned to him. At first Nils was hesitant, but the man was smiling. He spread a lovely piece of satin damask on the counter.

Nils shook his head, thinking to himself, "I'll never be rich enough to buy any of that cloth."

Suddenly, Nils was the center of everyone's attention, all along the street. Wherever he looked a shopkeeper hurriedly displayed his wares, trembling with eagerness. Why, one of the merchants jumped over the counter, took him by the arm, and spread silver cloth and woven tapestries that shone with brilliant colors. Nils had to laugh. How could such a man suppose that he could buy such things?

Then the merchant showed him a tiny, worn coin—one much like the one that Nils had kicked out of his way before he

entered the city. To the boy's surprise, the merchant added a pair of large, heavy, silver goblets to his pile of fine cloth.

Would he actually sell all of this treasure for so small a coin? Nils was perplexed. He began to dig down in his pockets for a coin, any coin.

When all the other merchants saw that he was looking for money, they offered him gold and silver ornaments. All they asked was one little penny.

Nils turned his vest and breeches pockets inside out. He had nothing, not even a penny. When he saw the tears in the merchants' eyes, those people who seemed so rich, he couldn't help feeling sorry for them.

Wait! Maybe he could find the rusty old coin outside the city wall. He ran and ran and ran, and finally he had gone through the great gate and was outside the city. Where was the little green copper penny that had lain on the strand?

He found it.

When he stood up, his little treasure clutched in his hand, the city was gone. Had it been a ghostly trick, a dream, a hallucination?

Herr Ermenrich came up to him. Nils didn't hear him, and the stork had to poke the boy with his bill to attract his attention.

"What's the matter, my little tomten? Have you fallen asleep on your feet?"

"Oh, Herr Ermenrich!" exclaimed the boy, "did you see the city?"

"You must have been dreaming," the stork replied.

"No! No! I have not been dreaming," Nils insisted, and he told the stork everything that had happened.

Herr Ermenrich said, "Most likely you were dreaming, yet I will admit that Bataki the raven—who is the most learned of all birds—once told me that there used to be a city on this shore. It was called Vineta. It was so rich and so wonderful that its inhabitants became arrogant. As a punishment, the raven said, the city was flooded and sank into the sea.

"The people of that city cannot die, nor can their city be destroyed. One night, every one hundred years, the city rises in all its splendor and remains on the surface of the sea for one hour."

"Yes! That was the city I saw!" cried his little companion.

"When the hour is up, the city will sink again into the sea unless a merchant of Vineta manages to sell something—anything—to a living creature. Thumbietot, if you had had a coin—the very smallest coin—to pay the merchants, Vineta might have remained here on the shore; its people could have lived and died like other human beings."

"Herr Ermenrich," Nils said, tears streaming down his cheeks, "now I understand why you flew so far to find me in the middle of the night. You believed that I could save the city."

He covered his face with his hands and sobbed, and Herr Ermenrich looked as distressed as a stork could look.

Two Cities

The Living City

Monday, April eleventh.

Easter Monday afternoon, the wild geese and Thumbietot were on the wing over Gottland. The large island lay smooth and even beneath them. The ground was checked just as it was in Skåne; but there were only a few houses and no large manors with ancient castles, and there were more meadows among the fields.

The wild geese had taken the route over Gottland on account of Thumbietot. The boy had been grieving for two days, thinking only of his failure to break the curse on Vineta and the sad fate of its inhabitants.

Akka and the goosey-gander had tried to convince Thumbietot that he had only been dreaming, but he was so positive that what he had seen was real that he would not listen to them.

Then old Kaksi came back to the flock. She had been blown toward Gottland during the storm and had to travel over the whole island before she learned through some crows that her comrades were safe on Little Karl's Island.

When she heard Thumbietot's story of the city beneath the sea, she suggested, "Come with me, and I'll take you to a place that I saw yesterday. You will not be distressed very long."

In spite of his sadness, the boy was ready to travel on with his friends. What did Kaksi want him to see?

Now from his perch on Morton Goosey-Gander, high over the island of Gottland, the boy saw white lime walls with caves and crags, but most of the island was fairly level. This was a pleasant and peaceful Easter holiday afternoon. Trees were budding, and spring blossoms dressed the ground in the leafy meadows.

People were outdoors, enjoying the mild spring weather. Little children played ring games and sang as they played. The Salvation Army was out. Nils saw a lot of people dressed in the dark-blue and bright-red uniforms of the Army. They were sitting on a wooded hill, playing guitars and brass instruments, and singing gospel songs.

On one of the roads was a crowd of Good Templars who were on a pleasure trip. He recognized them by the gold inscriptions on the big banners they were carrying. They sang song after song, for as long as he could hear them.

The boy had been observing the panorama below him for quite a while. Now he looked up. There, right in front of him, was the western coast of the island, the wide, blue sea...and a remarkable city on the shore. The sun had just begun to go down, so Nils couldn't see the city very well. Its walls and towers and high, gabled houses and churches stood there perfectly black against the light evening sky. For a few moments, he believed that this city was just as beautiful as the city he had seen on Easter night.

When he got right up to it, he saw that it was both like and unlike the city beneath the sea. Once upon a time, this city must have been enclosed by a wall with towers and gates; but the towers were roofless, hollow and empty. The gates no longer had doors. The sentinels and warriors had left. All the glittering splendor was gone.

As the geese flew over, Nils saw what was left of little houses and high, gabled ones; and there were still a few cathedrals from the old days. The walls of the gabled houses were whitewashed, but the boy could imagine how they had once been decorated. In all the buildings, windows were empty, the floors were grass-grown, and ivy climbed along the walls.

The narrow streets were deserted. Stately people had once sauntered along them. There had been workshops filled with all sorts of skilled workmen, merchants, and fine wares.

But there was also something very important that the boy did not see—that the city was *still* both beautiful and remarkable. He did not notice the cheery cottages on the side streets, nor the pretty gardens and avenues, not even the beauty in the weed-clad ruins. He was so wrapped up in the past that he could not see good in the present.

Finally the wild geese sank down to the grass-grown floor of a cathedral ruin to spend the night. As they arranged themselves for sleep, the boy looked up through the open arches, to the pale-pink evening sky. After awhile, he decided that he was tired of grieving for the old city under the sea.

If he had broken the spell, the city would eventually have become as broken-down and deserted as this one.

"If I had the power to save the city, I don't think that I would do it. I would rather have it remain in all its glory below the surface of the sea," he said to himself, and then he drifted off to sleep.

Many among the young may feel that something so great and grand should always be their heart's desire. Older people, who have learned the value of modesty and are satisfied with what they have, are more happy with the Visby that exists than the magnificent Vineta at the bottom of the sea.

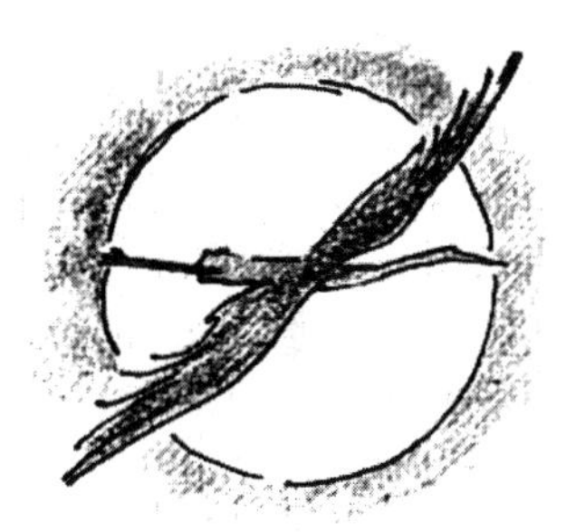

THE TRAVELS OF
BOOK ONE
NILS HOLGERSSON

Chapter Fifteen

The Legend of Småland

Tuesday, April twelfth.

Early in the evening, the wild geese arrived in Tjust Township, in northern Småland. Under the soft peach and turquoise sky Nils could see islands and peninsulas and points and capes among shimmering fjords. Beyond the tree-lined shores, there were fields; and at the tops of the little hills there were more trees. Here and there on the islands were cabins and cottages. Farther inland were larger dwellings, and farthest inland were large, white manors.

"What a pretty place," the boy thought.

The geese alighted on a limestone island in Goose-fjord. With Akka's first glance at the shore, she observed that spring was well on its way in Småland. Although the trees were still winter-bare, the ground beneath them was brocaded with both white and blue anemones.

"We haven't time to tour Småland, I'm afraid," the lead goose told her fellow travelers. "By tomorrow morning we must travel north, over Östergötland."

Nils said nothing, but he was disappointed. Last summer, when he was tending geese for a farmer in the neighborhood of Jordberga, he had met two Småland children, and they had told him the legend of Småland. Of course he hadn't believed their tale, but he would've liked to have seen the province himself.

"Have you heard, Nils, how God created Skåne and Småland?" Little Mats, the younger of the two children, had asked.

"No," Nils had replied.

"Well, way back when God was creating the world, He was doing his best work on Småland."

"Oh, of course," Nils interrupted. "He would be doing his best work there since you and your sister, Osa, were born there, Mats."

"Ya, sure," the boy answered with a grin, and continued:

"Saint Peter came by, and he stopped and looked.

"'Say,' he said, 'is that hard to do?'

"'It isn't easy,' the Lord replied.'

"Saint Peter stood looking awhile, and then he said, 'God, why don't you take a rest? I'll take over.'

"'I don't think that would be a good idea, Saint Peter. You haven't had any experience.'

"'I've been watching,' the old saint huffed. 'I could do as well as you've done.'

"God looked worried, but then he relented. The northern and eastern parts of Småland were already beautiful and fertile. No one, not even Saint Peter, could ruin the land.

"'Go ahead, then, Saint Peter. I will begin work on Skåne while you finish Småland.'

"In a few minutes Saint Peter was again looking over God's shoulder. The saint had to admit that Skåne was a good piece of workmanship. It was a fertile land, easy to cultivate, with wide plains and hardly any hills.

"'Yes, that's nice,' Saint Peter said, 'but Småland is much nicer.'

"'Have you finished already?' God asked.

"'A long time ago,' Saint Peter said, and the two of them walked over to the Swedish province.

"'What have you done!' God exclaimed when he saw it.

"Saint Peter was horrified. He had had the idea that if he heaped rocks in a pile and covered them with a thin layer of top-

soil, the land would become a tropical paradise. After all, he had reasoned, the mountain would receive all the benefits of the sun's warm, life-giving rays.

"But while he was talking to God, a fierce cloudburst had washed the topsoil away, leaving the rock pile. The best that the southern, western and interior parts of Småland could boast were places where clay and heavy gravel lay on the rocks. Only spruce and juniper, moss and heather could grow there.

"Water had filled all the clefts in the mountain, and there were lakes and rivers and brooks everywhere, not to mention swamps. Most places had too much water. If that weren't bad enough, other areas had little or no water at all.

"'I wanted a tropical paradise,' Saint Peter moaned, 'so I constructed a land near the sun.'

"'The night chill also comes from heaven,' God reminded him. 'This part of Småland will be frost-bound; it can't be helped.'"

At this point in the story, Mat's sister, Osa, had protested: "You're not being fair. You'll never find richer grain farming than in Möre district, by Kalmar Sound. Why, there are fields upon fields, just like here in Skåne."

"I can't help that," her brother said. "I'm just repeating what I've heard others say."

"Well, little Mats, I have heard many people say that Tjust is one of the most beautiful coastlands on earth. Think of the bays and islets, and the manors, and the groves."

"Yes, that's true," Mats agreed.

"Don't you remember your schoolteacher telling you that no place in Sweden could compare with Småland just south of Lake Vettern?"

"Oh, well…" little Mats said.

"Think of Visingsö, with the ruins and the oak forests. And think of the Emån River Valley, with all the villages and flour mills, sawmills, and carpenter shops."

Little Mats screwed up his face and thought.

"Oho!" he said. "Don't you see? Everything good was in the part that God made. Saint Peter's Småland was a wreck. No wonder God was upset!

"God said, 'Saint Peter, I'll have to make the Smålanders especially smart, thrifty and enterprising; otherwise they will never be able to exist in this country. You make the Skåninge.'"

"Wait a minute!" Nils interrupted. "What makes you think Saint Peter could create the Skåninge as well as God could create the Smålanders?"

"I don't."

"Aargh!"

Nils was about to thrash little Mats, when Osa sprang like a lioness to help her little brother. Nils Holgersson had no intention of fighting a girl, so he let Mats go. Then he ignored the two Småland children for the rest of the day.

THE TRAVELS OF
BOOK ONE
NILS HOLGERSSON

Chapter Sixteen

The Crows

The Clay Crock

Sonnerbo Township lies in the southwestern corner of Småland. If you saw it in the wintertime, you would probably think that the snow was covering garden plots, rye fields, and clover meadows. After all, most flat areas in Sweden are fertile and cultivated. Sonnerbo is different. If you could see the township in early April, when the snow finally melts there, you would realize that the land is dry, sandy, and rocky in some areas and swampy in others. Oh, there are fields, but they are small. There are little red or gray farmhouses, too, but not very many of them.

Right where Sonnerbo touches the boundary of Halland, there's a sandy heath. The heath is so large that if you stood on one side of it, you wouldn't be able to see across to the other side. Nothing but heather grows there; perhaps nothing else could grow there. The only place that's not overgrown with heather is a low, stony ridge. Crows call it Crow Ridge. On that ridge are juniper bushes, mountain ash, a few oaks; oh, yes, and there is a little cabin there.

When Nils Holgersson was traveling with the wild geese, the cabin was empty. The people who had lived there had closed the damper, fastened the window hooks, and locked the door. They had forgotten one thing, though, and that was to repair the broken windowpane.

Two summers went by, and the rag that had kept wind and rain from blowing through the broken windowpane shrank, and a crow knocked it out. That crow was one of hundreds in the area. Naturally the crows did not live there all year round. During the summer they lived on eggs, berries and fledgling birds throughout Sonnerbo Township. In the autumn they flew from one field to another, all over Götaland, picking grain. When winter was over and spring triggered their nesting instinct, the crows returned to Sonnerbo's heather heath near the little cabin.

Garm Whitefeather was the name of the crow who had poked the rag out of the window, but Garm was generally called Fumle-Drumle because he was so clumsy and stupid. This crow was singularly unfortunate. He came from good stock; in fact, he should have been chieftain of the crows. After all, this honor had from time immemorial belonged to the oldest Whitefeather. Long before Garm Whitefeather was born, however, the power had been transferred to a cruel crow named Wind-Rush.

The crows, conspiring among themselves, had decided to improve their own lifestyle by stealing from others, especially the defenseless. They began by murdering their chieftain, an admirable crow with an excellent reputation among birds and beasts and men. The traitors chose a notorious robber to be their leader and, in only a short time, became even more feared than pigeon hawks and leech owls. The wicked crows attacked baby hares and small birds, and plundered birds' nests.

Strangely, the last member of the chieftain stock became Wind-Rush's court jester. Wind-Rush liked to take Fumle-Drumle along on hunting expeditions because the fool's bungling efforts made his own exploits seem skillful and daring.

None of the crows knew that Fumle-Drumle had pecked the rag out of the cabin window. Anyway, they would never have believed that he had the courage to approach a human being's dwelling. Garm kept his thoughts to himself, not once mentioning that the cabin was open. He had good reason.

Wind-Rush treated Garm Whitefeather reasonably well in the daytime, when others could see. The rebel chieftain showed

his true hatred only in darkness. One pitch-black night, when the Whitefeather stood on his night perch, he was attacked by two crows and almost murdered. From then on, after dark Garm would silently slip away from his usual night perch and fly to the cabin.

One afternoon, when the crows were up to their usual mischief, they flew down into a gravel pit.

"Why did the humans dig that pit?" they cawed among themselves. To satisfy their insatiable curiosity, they turned every single grain of sand to find out. While the crows were hopping around down there, a wall of the pit caved in. They rushed over to look at it, and they found a large clay crock. Of course they wanted to know what was in it; but to their disappointment, it was fastened shut. They tried to peck holes in the pottery, but it was too hard to pierce. Then they tried to bend the wooden clasp, but they couldn't do that either.

"Do you crows need some help?"

They glanced up quickly. A fox sat on the edge of the gravel pit. He was one of the prettiest foxes they had ever seen, except that he had lost an ear.

"Oh, well, if you're inclined to help, we won't stop you," Wind-Rush said.

The crows flew out of the gravel pit, and Smirre Fox climbed in. He bit at the jar and pulled at the lock, but he couldn't open it.

"Can you tell what's in the crock?" Wind-Rush called down.

Smirre rolled the crock back and forth, listening closely. "I think there's silver money in it," he replied.

"Do you really think so?" The crows looked greedily at the crock, because there's nothing crows love more than silver money.

"Listen to the crock rattle when I roll it," Smirre said, and he gave it a shove. "Only I don't know how to get at the money."

Disgusted, Wind-Rush said, "There's no way to get it out."

The fox stood and rubbed his head against his left foreleg and thought. A bright idea popped into his head. Maybe this, at last, was his chance to get revenge on that little imp, Thumbietot.

"Say," he said, "I think I know someone who could open this crock for you."

"Tell us! Tell us!" the crows cried, so excited that they prac-

tically tumbled down into the pit.

"Thumbietot, the tomten, can do it," the fox said. "All you have to do is bring him here."

"Why are you telling us this? What do you expect to get in return for your information?" Wind-Rush asked suspiciously.

"I want Thumbietot, that's all," Smirre said.

Wind-Rush did not care about a little tomten, so he immediately agreed to the compact. Well, reaching an agreement with the fox was simple enough, but finding Thumbietot would not be easy. After saying they would soon return, Wind-Rush and fifty of his fastest crows flew off. Day after day passed, and still the crows on Crow Ridge saw no sign of their leader.

Kidnapped by Crows

Wednesday, April thirteenth.

The wild geese were up at daybreak so they could get a bite of food before starting out on the journey toward Östergötland. The island in Goosefjord, where they had slept, was barren. There was nothing for them to eat there, but they could eat the green seaweed growing in the water all around the little island.

Unfortunately for him, Nils couldn't eat seaweed. As he stood on the island's shore, hungry and drowsy, he looked in every direction for something to eat. His glance fell upon two squirrels who were playing on the wooded point directly across from the island. He wondered if the squirrels had any winter supplies remaining, and he asked the goosey-gander to take him over to the point so he could ask them for a couple of hazel nuts. Morton Goosey-Gander immediately swam across the sound with him.

The squirrels were having too much fun chasing about to stop and listen to the tiny boy. They ran farther into the forest, with him running after them. Soon Nils was out of the gander's sight, but the faithful friend patiently waited on shore.

Nils waded among white anemones, which were so high that they reached to his chin, when he felt someone grab him from behind and try to lift him up. He turned around and saw that a crow had him by the shirtband. He tried to break loose, but another crow gripped him by the stocking and knocked him over.

If Nils Holgersson had called for help immediately, the white goosey-gander certainly would have been able to save him; but the boy thought he could protect himself against two crows. He kicked and struck out; but the crows didn't lose their hold, and they soon had him in the tree tops. To make matters worse, they flew so recklessly that his head struck hard against a branch, and he lost consciousness.

When he opened his eyes once more, he found himself high above the ground. He had no idea how far he was from his friends, nor where the crazy crows were taking him. When he looked down, he saw what looked like a woolen carpet woven in greens and reds, in large irregular patterns. Long tears ran through it; in some places, large pieces had been ripped away. Oddest of all, the carpet seemed to cover a mirror floor; for under the tears in the carpet shone bright, glittering glass.

Suddenly, the sun rose from the horizon, and the mirror shimmered in red and gold. Oh, the rich carpet and the sparkling glass beneath it were gorgeous! In spite of his desperate situation, Nils was delighted.

Then the crows flew lower, and he saw that the carpet was the earth, dressed in green and brown conifers and deciduous trees; the holes and tears were shining fjords and lakes. Where was he? Nils wondered, still faint from his rap on the head. Why were crows swarming around him? Why was he being pulled and knocked around so that he was about to break to pieces?

"Oh!" Nils exclaimed. He remembered. He had been kidnapped by crows. The white goosey-gander must still be waiting on the wooded point across from the island, and today the wild geese were going to travel to Östergötland. Nils was being carried southwest; he knew that because the sun was behind him. The big forest-carpet beneath him must be Småland.

"What will become of the goosey-gander now that I can't watch over him?" Nils groaned.

"Stop! Stop! Put me down!" he shouted. Nils wasn't exactly

afraid. He believed that the crows were carrying him off simply in a spirit of mischief. He didn't think they meant him any harm.

The crows ignored his cries and flew on as fast as they could. Then one flapped his wings in a way that meant "Look out! Danger!" They flew down into a spruce forest, pushing their way between prickly branches to the ground. They pushed the boy down under a thick spruce, where he was so hidden that not even a falcon could have sighted him. Fifty-one crows surrounded him.

"Why have you carried me off?" Nils demanded, but a big crow hissed, "Be quiet or I'll pick your eyes out!"

Nils sat there and stared at the crows, and they stared back at him. The longer he looked at them, the less he liked them. Their feathers were dusty and unkempt, their toes and claws were caked with dried mud, and the corners of their beaks were covered with food drippings. They had a cruel, sneaky appearance, like ruthless cutthroats.

"This must be a robber band," Nils thought. Then he heard the familiar call, "Where are you? Here I am. Where are you? Here I am." Akka and the others had gone out in search for him.

Before he could answer them, the big crow who appeared to be the leader of the band hissed in his ear, "Think of your eyes!" He had to keep still. He heard the wild geese call again and again, but the sound grew fainter as they flew on.

"Well, now you're on your own, Nils Holgersson," the boy said to himself. "Now you can prove whether or not you've learned anything in the weeks you've spent in the open."

When the crows were about to take off into the air again, Nils shouted, "Isn't there a single one of you who's strong enough to carry me on his back? I won't jump off. I promise!"

"Be quiet!" a crow commanded.

"Oh, uh, Wind-Rush… Oh, uh, fearless leader…"

Nils turned to look at the crow who hopped up to the big crow. Why, this crow was even bigger than the leader; and he was even messier, and so clumsy-looking that the boy had to laugh.

"What!" the leader snapped.

"Oh, um, um, wouldn't it be better, Wind-Rush, if Thumbietot got there whole rather than in half? I could carry him on my back."

"If you can do it, Fumle-Drumle, I have no objection," Wind-Rush said, "but don't lose him!"

Garm Whitefeather gently picked up the little tomten and put him on his back. The crows continued to fly southwest, over Småland. Birds down on the earth were singing their best love songs. In a high, dark forest, the thrush admired his sweetheart and began to sing, "How pretty you are! How pretty you are! How pretty you are!" As soon as he finished this tune, he started another: "No one is so pretty. No one is so pretty. No one is so pretty." Then he began all over again.

When Nils Thumbietot Holgersson realized that the thrush knew only two tunes, he shouted at him: "We've heard all this before. We've heard all this before."

"Who is it? Who is it? Who is it? Who makes fun of me?" the thrush asked, and tried to catch a glimpse of the little thing that was taunting him.

The crow chief said, "Be careful of your eyes, Thumbietot!" but the boy thought, "I'm going to show you that I'm not afraid of you!"

Farther and farther inland they traveled, and there were rivers and lakes everywhere. The wood dove and his lady dove sat on a branch in a birch grove. He blew up his feathers, cocked his head, raised and lowered his body, until the breast feathers vibrated against the branch. All the while he cooed to his mate: "Thou, thou, thou art the loveliest in all the forest. No one in the forest is as lovely as thou, thou, thou!"

Nils couldn't keep still. When he heard the dove, he cried out: "Don't you believe him! Don't you believe him!"

"Who, who, who is it that lies about me?" cooed the dove, and tried to see the one who slandered him.

"Caught-by-Crows lies about you!" shouted the boy.

Again the crow warned Nils, but Fumle-Drumle said: "Great leader, let him chatter. The little birds will think we crows are quick-witted and funny."

"They're not the fools you think they are," Wind-Rush said, but he went along with the idea, and he let the boy call out as much as he liked.

They flew mostly over forests, but there were churches and parishes and little cabins. In one place they saw a pretty old manor. The forest was behind it and the sea in front of it; it had red walls and a turreted roof, and there were great sycamores on the grounds and thick gooseberry bushes in the orchard. A starling sat on top of the weathercock, singing so loudly that every note was heard by the wife, who sat on an egg in the heart of a pear tree.

"We have four pretty little eggs," the starling sang. "We have four pretty, little, round eggs. We have the whole nest filled with fine eggs."

Nils cupped his hands over his mouth and shouted: "The magpie will get them! The magpie will get them!"

"Who wants to frighten me?" asked the starling, flapping his wings uneasily.

"Captured-by-Crows frightens you!" Nils replied. By this time the crow chief and his crew were having so much fun that they cawed with satisfaction.

The farther inland they flew, the larger the lakes became and the more plentiful the islands and points. On a lakeshore stood a drake who was kowtowing before his true love.

"I'll be true to you all the days of my life. I'll be true to you all the days of my life. I'll be true to you all the days of my life," the drake promised her.

"It won't last till the summer's end!" Nils shouted.

"Who are you?" called the offended drake.

"My name's Stolen-by-Crows," the boy answered.

At dinnertime the crows landed in a grove, where they found food. None of them thought of the boy. Then Fumle-Drumle dragged a dog-rose branch, with a few dried buds on it, up to the chief.

"Here's something for you, Wind-Rush," the fool said. "You'll like it."

Wind-Rush sniffed contemptuously. "Do you think I want to eat old, dry buds?" he asked.

"I thought you would be pleased," Fumle-Drumle said, throwing the branch in front of the boy. Nils grabbed the buds and ate them.

When the crows were full, they began to chatter. "What're you thinking about, Wind-Rush?" asked one. "You're so quiet."

"Oh, I'm thinking about a hen who once lived in this district. She was very fond of her mistress; and to please her, she laid a nest full of eggs, which she hid under the storehouse floor. The mistress of the house wondered where her hen was, but she couldn't find her. Can you guess, Longbill, who found her and the eggs?"

"Oho! I think I can guess, Wind-Rush," the crow answered. "Do you remember the big, black cat in Hinneryd's parish house? She was unhappy because the newborn kittens were always taken from her and drowned. Just once she succeeded in hiding them, and that was when she laid them in a haystack outside. She was pretty happy with those kittens, but I daresay I got more pleasure out of them than she did."

The crows became so excited that they all talked at once. "What kind of accomplishment is that—to steal little kittens?" bragged one. "I once chased a young hare who was almost full-grown." He got no farther in his tale before another interrupted, "Hah! I stole a silver spoon from a human being!"

"Listen to me, you evil crows!" Nils said. "You ought to be ashamed of yourselves. I have lived among wild geese for three weeks, and not once have I seen or heard anything but good. You must have a bad chief, since he allows you to rob and murder like this. If you don't mend your ways, human beings will root you out. There will soon be an end of you!"

Wind-Rush and the crows flew at him, but Fumle-Drumle stood in front of him, barring their way. He laughed and cawed, and then he seemed to cower.

"Oh, no, no!" he said. "What will Wind-Air say if you tear Thumbietot into pieces before he has gotten the silver pieces for us?"

"I'd expect you to be afraid of women, Fumle-Drumle," said the crow chieftain. At any rate, he and the others left Nils alone.

The crows took to the air again. The boy had begun to think that Småland was far more beautiful and fertile than he had been told. Of course it was wooded and full of mountain ridges, but cultivated grounds lay alongside the islands and lakes. The farther inland he went, though, he saw fewer and fewer villages and cottages. Finally he saw nothing but swamps, heaths and juniper hills.

The sun had gone down, but the sky was still light when the crows reached the large heather heath. Wind-Rush sent a crow on ahead to say that he had been successful. Within a few minutes, Wind-Air and several hundred crows from Crow Ridge came to meet them.

In the midst of the deafening cawing, Fumle-Drumle said to the boy: "You've been so comical during the trip that I've become really fond of you. I'll give you some good advice. As soon as we land, you will be told to do a bit of work that may seem easy to you. Beware of doing it!"

Before long, Fumle-Drumle put Nils down in the bottom of a sandpit. The boy fell down, rolled over, and lay there on the ground as though he were exhausted. So many crows hovered around him that the air rushing through their wings howled like a windstorm, but he didn't look up.

"Thumbietot, get up!" Wind-Rush commanded. "I have something easy for you to do."

The boy pretended to be asleep. Then Wind-Rush took him by the arm and dragged him over the sand to the clay crock.

"Open the crock!" Wind-Rush said, shaking him.

"How could I, just a poor little boy, open that crock? Why, it's every bit as big as I am!"

"Open it, I said!" Wind-Rush commanded once more. "Open it, or you'll be sorry you didn't!"

The boy got up, tottered over to the crock, fumbled with the clasp, and said, "I'm not usually so weak. Let me sleep until morning. Then I think I could get the clasp to open."

Wind-Rush pinched the boy's leg with his beak. Nils jerked himself free, ran a few paces backward, drew his knife from the sheath, and brandished it.

"You'd better be careful!" he warned the crow.

Wind-Rush flew at him in a blind rage, straight toward the knife, which plunged through his eye into his head. Nils drew the knife back quickly, but Wind-Rush only struck out with his wings and then fell down—dead.

"Wind-Rush is dead! The stranger has killed our chieftain!" the crows screeched. Some wailed. Others cried for vengeance. Fumle-Drumle spread his wings over the boy, preventing the others

from running their bills into him.

Nils knew he couldn't escape…unless… He took a firm hold on the clasp of the crock and pulled it off. Then he hopped inside. No, that wasn't such a good hiding place. The crock was nearly filled to the brim with thin silver coins. The boy began to throw out the coins.

Immediately the crows forgot their thirst for vengeance. They scurried to collect the money. Even Wind-Air scooped it up. Every crow who succeeded in picking up a coin flew off to the nest to conceal it.

When the coins were gone, Nils looked up. Only one crow was in the sandpit now. That was Fumle-Drumle.

"You have rendered me a greater service than you could understand," the crow said—with a very different tone of voice—"and I want to save your life. Climb on my back, and I'll take you to a hiding place where you'll be safe for tonight. Tomorrow I'll make arrangements for you to return to the wild geese."

The Cabin

Thursday, April fourteenth.

The following morning when the boy awoke, he was lying in a bed. At first he thought that he was at home and muttered to himself, half-awake, "I wonder if Mother will bring me coffee."

Then he remembered that he was in a deserted cabin on Crow Ridge and that Fumle-Drumle, the crow with the white feather, had borne him there. The boy was sore all over after the journey he had made the day before, and he thought it was lovely to lie still while he waited for Fumle-Drumle, who had promised to come and get him.

Curtains of checked cloth hung before the bed, and he drew them aside to look out into the cabin. Why, he had never seen a cabin like this. The walls were no higher than a couple of logs laid horizontally. There was no interior ceiling, so he could look clear up to the roof-tree. The cabin was so small that it seemed to have been built for tomtens, not real people; but the fireplace and chimney were as large as any he had ever seen. Even the entrance, in a gable wall at the side of the fireplace, was almost too narrow for a grown human being. In the other gable wall he saw a low, wide window with many panes. There was scarcely any movable furniture in the cabin; the bench on one side and the table under the window were stationary, as were the cupboard and the big bed where he lie.

"Who owns the cabin?" Nils wondered aloud. "The people who lived here must have expected to return."

The coffee urn and the gruel pot stood on the hearth, and there was wood in the fireplace. The oven rake and the baker's peel stood in a corner. The spinning wheel was raised on a bench. Oakum and flax, a couple of skeins of yarn, a candle, and a bunch of matches were on the shelf over the window. There were bedclothes on the bed; and on the walls there still hung long strips of cloth, upon which three legendary wisemen named Caspar, Melchior, and Balthazar were painted. They and their handsome steeds were pictured many times. They rode around the whole cabin and continued their ride even up toward the joists in the roof.

In the roof the boy saw something that made him wide awake. Two big loaves of bread cakes hung there on a spit. They looked old and moldy, but Nils was too hungry to care. He poked at them with an oven rake, and a piece fell to the floor. He ate some of it and put the rest into his bag. Then he looked around the cabin once more to try and find anything else that might be useful.

"I may as well take what I need, since no one else cares," he thought. Most of the things were too big and heavy for him. He did see some matches, though. To get them, he climbed up onto the table, grabbed hold of the window curtains, and swung up to the window shelf. He managed to stuff a few matches into his bag. While he stood there, the crow with the white feather came in through the window.

"Well, here I am at last," the crow said as he lit on the table. "I couldn't get here any sooner because we crows have elected a new chieftain."

"Who was chosen?" Nils asked.

"A crow who will not allow robbery and injustice. A crow by the name of Garm Whitefeather," he said, pausing. "A crow who was, until last night, called Fumle-Drumle." He drew himself up until he looked absolutely regal.

"That was a good choice," Nils said, and he congratulated him.

"Wish me luck," the crow said, and he told the boy all about the election.

"Is he in there?"

The boy thought he heard a familiar voice.

"Yes, he's hidden in there," answered a crow voice.

"Be careful, Thumbietot!" Garm cried. "Wind-Air and that fox are outside the window."

Before he could say more, Smirre jumped through the window, smashing it, and killed Garm Whitefeather with a single swipe of his paw. Then the fox looked for the boy. Nils tried to hide behind a big spiral of oakum, but Smirre had already seen him and crouched for the final spring.

Nils struck a match, touched the curtains, and when they were in flames, threw them down on the fox. Wild with fear, Smirre ran out of the cabin. Nils was in even greater danger than before. The fire spread to the bed hangings. He jumped down and tried to smother it, but the cabin filled with smoke.

Meanwhile, Smirre Fox realized that he'd been more afraid than hurt. He snickered from just outside the window. "Thumbietot," he shouted, "Would you rather be fried in there or eaten out here? I would prefer to eat you, but whatever your choice, I'll be satisfied."

Nils thought the fox was right. He really had no choice at all. The whole bed was ablaze; smoke rolled across the floor, and fire crept along the painted wall strips, from rider to rider. The boy jumped into the fireplace and tried to open the oven door, when he heard a key turning in the lock. Human beings were coming! Nils was already on the threshold when the door opened. He saw two children facing him, but without a moment's thought, rushed past them into the open.

He didn't dare run far. He knew that Smirre Fox was waiting. The boy's only hope for survival was to stay near the children. He turned around to get a good look at them.

In pure astonishment, the little tomten shouted, "Oh, good morning, Osa goose-girl! Good morning, little Mats!"

Crows, the burning cabin, everything except those children had vanished from his memory. He might have been walking on a stubble field in West Vemminghög, tending a flock of geese. The two Småland children, he thought, would greet him as they would an old friend.

No, when the children saw the tiny creature running toward them with outstretched hands, they were frightened. Nils realized, with a sinking heart, that things would never be the same again. Ashamed, he turned and ran. He didn't know where he was going.

Down on the heath, he spied something white. There was Morton Goosey-Gander, and Dunfin was with him. When the goosey-gander saw the boy running so fast, he thought that something horrible must be pursuing him. The gander flung him onto his back and flew off with him.

THE TRAVELS OF
BOOK ONE
NILS HOLGERSSON

Chapter Seventeen

The Old Peasant Woman

Thursday, April fourteenth.

On a cold evening in Småland, three travelers were searching for a place to rest. They should have been able to find something; they did not require any luxury.

"If one of these long mountain ridges had a peak high enough and steep enough so that a fox could not reach it, we could rest there," said one.

"If a single swamp were thawed out enough so that a fox wouldn't dare venture out on it, that would be a good place to sleep," said the second.

"If the ice on any one of the lakes we pass were loose, so that a fox could not cross it, we would be safe there," said the third.

The worst of it was that when the sun had gone, two of the travelers became so sleepy that they could hardly stay awake. The third one grew more and more uneasy as darkness approached.

"What a misfortune it is that we have come to a land where the lakes and swamps are still frozen. Here in the very coldest part of Småland, spring has not yet come."

The shelter they needed seemed nowhere to be found on

this dark, chilly, drizzly night. For some reason, the travelers were unwilling to ask any farmers for lodging. They had already passed many parishes without knocking on a door.

When there was barely a glimmer of light left in the sky, they happened into a farmyard far away from neighbors. The buildings appeared to be uninhabited. No smoke rose from the chimney, no light shone through the windows, no human being moved on the place.

"Come what may, we'll have to stay here," decided the one who could stay awake. He looked around. This was not a small farm. Besides the house and stable and smokehouse, there were granaries, storehouses and cowsheds. All were old and rundown. The walls of the buildings were about to topple over, and they were covered with moss. There were yawning holes in the roofs, and the doors hung askew on broken hinges.

"There's the cowshed," said the leader of the trio, with relief. He roused his companions and conducted them to the cowshed door. Luckily the door was only fastened by a hook, which he easily pushed up with a rod.

"Are you coming at last, Mistress?" a cow bellowed. "I had begun to think you wouldn't bring me any supper tonight."

"We...we're poor travelers who want to find a place tonight where we'll be safe from a fox."

The cow rolled her eyes, twisted in her stall, and looked closely at the strangers.

"There's been no fox here, and there's room enough for the three of you," the cow mooed. "No one lives here except for an old peasant woman and myself. Who are you?"

"I am Nils Holgersson from Vemminghög, who has been turned into a tomten," replied the spokesman of the travelers. "With me are Morton Goosey-Gander, a tame goose, and Dunfin, a gray wild goose."

"Few guests have ever been within my four walls," mooed the cow, "and you are welcome although I would've been happier still to see my mistress come with my supper."

The boy led the geese into the large cowshed and then over to an empty manger. They fell sound asleep. For himself, he made a little bed of straw and thought that he, too, would go to sleep at once. The cow made that impossible. She shook her flanks, moved around in the stall, and complained of how hungry she was.

Nils lay thinking of what had happened to him in the past few days—of Osa the goose-girl and little Mats, whom he had encountered so unexpectedly. He wondered if the little cabin that he had set on fire had been their old home in Småland. Why, if that were so, then he had caused them trouble and unhappiness. If he ever became a human being again, he would try to compensate them for the damage he had done. Then he thought about Fumle-Drumle, the courageous crow who had saved his life and then been murdered so soon after he had been elected chieftain. Tears came to his eyes. What a stroke of luck it was that Morton Goosey-Gander and Dunfin found him!

The goosey-gander had told him that when the wild geese discovered he had disappeared, they asked the small birds of the forest if they had seen him. Ah, yes, the small birds knew that he had been taken by Småland crows, but they did not know where.

Then Akka had instructed the wild geese to search for Thumbietot in pairs. After a two-day hunt, whether or not they had found him, they were to meet in northwestern Småland on a high mountaintop called Taberg. After she had explained how to get to Taberg, the birds began their search.

The white goosey-gander had chosen Dunfin as his traveling companion, and they had flown here and there until they came upon a thrush wailing that a stranger named Kidnapped-by-Crows had made fun of him. When the geese asked, "Which way did the stranger go?" the thrush pointed, and they flew off in that direction. They met a dove cock, a starling, and a drake who were complaining about a little culprit who had disturbed their songs. The birds called him Caught-by-Crows, Captured-by-Crows, and Stolen-by-Crows. By listening for complaining voices and asking questions, Morton Goosey-Gander and Dunfin traced the boy all the way to the heather heath in Sonnerbo Township.

After the two geese had found him, they had taken off for Taberg, but the mountain was too far away for them to reach before darkness.

"If only we reach Taberg tomorrow, we'll be safe at last," murmured the boy to himself. He cuddled down in the straw.

"What is wrong?" fumed the cow. "I haven't been milked and I have no night fodder. My mistress came here at dusk to put things in order for me, but she became ill and went back to the house. She hasn't returned. What...what...oh, what can have happened? Moo! Moo! Moo!"

The boy realized that he was not going to get any rest in the cowshed. He rolled over and said to the cow, "Why are you telling me all this? I don't think I could help you. I'm too little!"

"What? Too little? All the little tomten I've ever heard of

could pull a whole load of hay and strike a cow dead with one fist!"

Nils couldn't help laughing. Where did the cow hear such a story? "Those tomten were quite different from me," he said. "I can do something for you, though. I'll loosen your halter and open the door for you. Then you can go out and drink from a

puddle of rainwater. While you're out, I'll climb up to the hayloft and throw hay into your manger."

"That would help, thank you," said the cow, and she quit bawling.

The boy did what he had said. When the cow was quietly eating, he thought that now, at last, he could get some sleep.

"Oh, oh, little tomten," mooed the cow.

"What?" he said, sleepily.

"May I ask one more thing?"

"Ya, ya," Nils said.

"Go to the cabin and find out what is wrong. I'm worried about my mistress."

"I can't show myself to human beings," the boy protested.

"Moo, moo, oh my, you can't be afraid of an old lady," said the cow. "She wouldn't harm you. Stand outside and look in through the crack in the door."

"Well, I would do that for you, of course," Nils said. He opened the cowshed door and went out into the yard. What a dark, cold, windy, rainy night! The worst of it was that seven big owls sat in a row on the eaves of the cabin, grumbling about the weather. What would happen to him if they saw him? Twice he was blown down before he got to the house. Once the wind swept him into a mud puddle so deep that he almost drowned. Anyway, he got to the house.

The cabin door was closed, but down in one corner a square had been cut out so that a cat could go in and out. Nils easily saw what was inside the cabin, and what he saw made him stagger back. An old, grayhaired woman was stretched out on the floor. She neither moved nor moaned, and her face was strangely white.

"She's dead!" Nils caught his breath. "Oh! I'm here with the dead...alone...at night!"

Nils ran back to the cowshed. When he told the cow what he saw, she stopped eating. "My mistress is dead? No-o-o! Moo! No-o-o! What will happen to me?"

"Someone will come and watch over you," the boy said to comfort her.

"No-o-o, you don't understand. I am twice as old as a cow usually is when she's taken to the slaughterhouse. But now, when I think that my poor mistress is dead, I have no desire to live any longer either.

"Is she lying on the bare floor?"

"Yes," the boy said.

"She used to come out here to the cowshed and talk about everything that troubled her. For the past few days, she has been afraid that she would die alone, with no one to close her eyes and fold her hands across her chest. Would...would you do that for her?"

Nils hesitated. He remembered that when his grandfather had died, his mother was careful to do that for him. On the other hand, he was afraid to be alone with a dead person on a dark night.

When the boy did not answer her, the cow did not repeat her request. Instead, she began to tell him about her mistress.

There was much to tell. She had many children. When they were little, they were in the cowshed every day, and in the summer they had taken the cattle to pasture in the swamp and in the groves, so the old cow knew all about them. The children had been happy, and they were good workers.

There was plenty to say about the farm itself, too. The buildings had not always been in shambles. The acreage was quite large, even though a fair amount of the land was either swampy or rocky and wooded. There was not much room for fields, but there was plenty of good fodder everywhere. At one time there had been a cow for every stall in the cowshed; and the oxshed, which was now empty, had once been filled with oxen. In those days, the mistress was happy. She would hum and sing when she entered the cowshed, and the cows lowed with gladness when they heard her coming.

The master of the farm died when the children were too small to help their mother. She had to take charge of the farm, with all the work and responsibility. In the evenings, when she came into the cowshed to milk, sometimes she was so tired that she wept.

"It doesn't matter," she would say, wiping her eyes. She became cheerful again. "No, it doesn't matter. Good times will come again when my children grow up. Oh, how I look forward to the future when my children can help me."

But as soon as the children were grown, they went away. They never helped their mother. Two of them were married before they left home; strangely, they left their little ones with the old mother. The grandchildren tended the cows just as their parents had done. And, in the evenings, when the mistress was so tired that she almost fell asleep milking the cows, she would rouse herself and say, "Good times will come again when my grandchildren grow up—yes, when my grandchildren grow up."

Then when these children grew up, they went to their parents far away. None stayed home. No one came back. The

old mistress was left alone on the farm.

"Do you think, Rödlinna, that I would ask them to stay here with me when they could go out in the world and make a better life for themselves? No," the old lady said to her old cow. "They would have only poverty to look forward to."

When the last grandchild was gone, the mistress lost interest in life. All at once she became bent and gray, and she tottered as she walked. She stopped working. She did not care to look after the farm, but let everything go to rack and ruin. She didn't repair the houses, and she sold the cows and oxen. The only cow that she kept was the old one who was now talking with Thumbietot.

The old mistress could have hired maids and farmhands, but she couldn't bear to see strangers do what her children and grandchildren might have done. She thought, "If my own children don't want this farm, it might as well fall into disrepair." She did not mind becoming poor; you see, she didn't value what was only hers. Yet she was afraid that her children might hear that she was destitute, and she didn't want to worry them.

Her children and grandchildren sent letters. They begged her to leave the farm and go live with them, but—how sad!—she didn't want to see the world that had taken her children from her.

She thought only of her children. When summer came, she led the cow out to graze in the big swamp. All day she would sit on the edge of the swamp, her hands in her lap. On the way home, she would say: "Rödlinna, if there had been large, rich fields here, there wouldn't have been any reason for my dear children to leave."

This evening she had been trembling. She could not even milk her cow, Rödlinna. She leaned against the manger and talked about two strangers who had asked if they might buy the swamp. They wanted to drain it, then sow and raise grain on it.

"Rödlinna, they said that grain can grow in the swamp! Do you hear? I'll write to the children and tell them to come home. Now they can come home. Rödlinna, do you hear?"

"That was what my dear mistress had gone to do, when suddenly she became very faint and trembling. That was what she had gone to do—"

Before she could say another word, the boy had opened the cowshed door and gone across the yard to the house. When he was inside, he saw that the house contained beautiful things; why, they were from America. The old lady's relatives had sent her a beautiful rocking chair. On the table under the window was a brocaded plush cover. There was a pretty spread on the bed. On the walls, in carved-wood frames, hung the photographs of the children and grandchildren who had gone away. On the bureau stood high vases and a couple of candlesticks with thick, spiral candles in them.

The boy found a box of matches, and then he lighted the candles; the lighted candles, he thought, would be one way to honor the dead. Then he went up to her, closed her eyes, folded her hands across her chest, and stroked the thin gray hair from her forehead.

Nils was no longer afraid of her, but he was deeply grieved because she had lived out her old age in loneliness and longing. He, at least, would watch over her dead body tonight. He hunted up the psalm book and seated himself to read a couple of psalms in an undertone.

In the middle of the reading, he paused. He had begun to think of his mother and father. Could they be longing for him as this poor old mother had longed for her children so far away in America? The thought made him happy and sad at once.

He hadn't been a good boy, but perhaps he could become one. Around him he saw photographs of men who had strong, earnest-looking faces. There were brides in long veils, gentlemen in fine clothes, and children with waved hair and pretty white dresses.

Nils looked closely. "Why, they seem to be staring blindly, as though they didn't want to see.

"Poor you!" he said to the portraits. "Your mother is dead. You cannot make amends now. You went away. My mother is living!" He paused, and nodded, and smiled to himself. "Both my father and my mother are living."

THE TRAVELS OF
BOOK ONE
NILS HOLGERSSON

Chapter Eighteen

From Taberg to Huskvarna

Friday, April fifteenth.

The boy sat awake most of the night, but toward morning he finally drifted off to sleep. Then he dreamed that he could hardly recognize his father and mother. Their hair was gray, and their skin was wrinkled! When he asked how they could have aged so prematurely, they said their longing for him had made them old. Why, Nils had expected them to be glad they were rid of him!

When the boy awoke, morning had come, bringing with it fine, clear weather. After eating a piece of bread that he had found in the cabin, he gave morning feed to the two geese and the cow. Then he opened the cowshed door so that the cow could go over to the nearest farm. Surely the neighbors would think something was wrong when they saw her wandering by herself. They would hurry to the rundown farm to see how the old woman was getting along, find her on the floor, and make proper funeral arrangements.

The three companions had barely become airborne when they saw what they had been looking for—Taberg, a high mountain with almost vertical walls and an abrupt, broken-off top. At the summit stood Akka, Yksi and Kaksi, Kolmi and Neljä, Viisi and Knusi, and all six goslings. They were waiting. When they saw that Dunfin and Morton had succeeded in finding Thumbietot, there was such a jubilant cackling and a fluttering and a calling that it could not be described.

After Nils had greeted his friends, he glanced around to get his bearings. The highest peak of Taberg, where he stood, was barren. To the east, south, and west, all he could see were dark spruce trees, brown bogs, ice-clad lakes, and blue mountain ridges. This land seemed to have been thrown together without much thought.

The land to the north was different; this had been created with the utmost care and affection. The boy could see majestic mountains, fertile valleys, and winding rivers, all the way to Lake Vettern. The big lake was ice-free and transparent, and its water was a remarkable blue color, as though the lake basin was full of blue light instead of water. Along the shore, a pale-blue mist enveloped the groves and hills and the roofs and spires of Jönköping City.

Later in the day, when the geese continued their journey, they flew up toward the blue valley. They were in high spirits. No one with ears could help hearing their happy shrieks. This was the first really fine spring day they had had in this part of the country.

The first ones to see the wild geese were miners on Taberg, who were drilling for ore at the mouth of a mine. When they heard the geese cackle, they paused in their drilling, and one of them called out, "Where are you going?"

The birds, of course, could not understand what the miner said, but Nils did. He replied, "Where there is neither pick nor hammer! That is where we are going!"

The miners, who felt the spring in the air and the longing to fly free like the wild geese, thought they only imagined that the reply was in human speech. Half-joking they cried, "Take us with you!"

"Not this year!" shouted the boy. "Not this year!"

The wild geese followed Taberg River down toward Monk Lake. Here, on the narrow strip of land between Monk and Vettern lakes, they saw Jönköping. First, the wild geese flew over Monksjö paper mills. The noon lunch hour was over, and workers were streaming down to the mill gate. When they heard the wild geese, they stopped a moment to listen. Some called, "Where are you going?"

The little Thumbietot answered for his traveling companions: "Where there are neither machines nor steam furnaces. That is where we are going!"

The paper mill workers thought their own longing made them imagine that the geese answered in human speech. "Take us with you!" they shouted back.

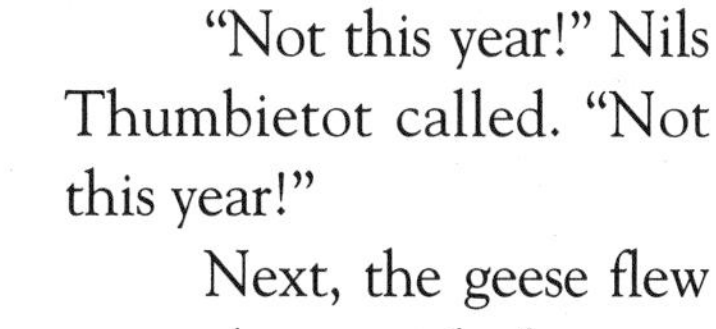

"Not this year!" Nils Thumbietot called. "Not this year!"

Next, the geese flew over the match factory, which lies on the shores of Vettern—large as a fortress—and lifts its high chimneys toward the sky. In one of the large workrooms, young women sat and filled matchboxes. The one who sat closest to an open window heard the cackles and shrieks of the wild geese. She leaned out with a matchbox in her hand and cried, "Where are you going?"

"To a land where there is no need of light or matches," the tiny tomten answered.

"Did the birds answer me?" the girl wondered. "No, of course not. All I heard was the cackling of the geese." Yet she could not refrain from calling, "Please, take me with you!"

"Not this year! Not this year!"

Jönköping stands east of the paper mill and the matchbox factory, with mountains to the left and to the right, with Monk Lake behind it and Vettern in front of it. The wild geese flew over the long, narrow city, but no one in the city answered their calls. The city folks never stopped to listen.

After awhile, the geese came to Sanna Sanitarium, farther along Vettern's shores. Some of the patients had gone out on the veranda to enjoy the spring air. One of them called feebly, "Where are you going?"

"Where there is neither sorrow nor sickness!" Thumbietot shouted.

"Oh, take us with you!" the patients pled.

"No, not this year. Not this year!" were the words they heard amid the cackling of the geese.

On and on the wild geese flew, until they came to Huskvarna. There it was—in a valley, with steep mountains all around it. Just as the geese flew overhead, a bell rang and a crowd of schoolchildren marched out into the schoolyard.

"Where are you going?" the schoolchildren shouted when they heard the wild geese.

"Where there are neither books nor lessons! That is where we are going!"

"Take us along!" the children replied.

"Not this year, but next," promised the tiny tomten they could not see. "Not this year, but next." He chuckled.

THE TRAVELS OF
BOOK ONE
NILS HOLGERSSON

Chapter Nineteen

The Big Bird Lake

The Wild Duck

Mount Omberg lies on the eastern shore of Vettern, Dagmosse lies east of Mount Omberg, and Lake Takern lies east of Dagmosse. The big, even Östergöta plain spreads around Lake Takern, as far as the eye can see.

Takern is a large lake. Long ago the lake was even larger, but people drained much of it for farming. Now the lake is a little more than six feet deep, but probably no more than seven feet deep anywhere. Little mud islands stick up here and there above the water's surface.

Reeds thrive upon the long, shallow Takern shores and around the little mud islands, growing over six feet high and so thick that pushing a boat through them is almost impossible. Only a few areas are clear for boating access. Among the reeds are little dams and canals with green, still water, where duckweed and pondweed grow, where gnat eggs and blackfish and worms hatch. Seabirds incubate their eggs and bring up their young there without being disturbed.

An incredible number of birds live among the Takern reeds. The first who settled there were the wild ducks, and they still live there by the thousands. They no longer own the entire lake, though; now they must share it with swans, grebes, coots, loons, fen ducks, and many other birds.

Some people say Takern is the largest and choicest bird lake in the whole country, but every so often a proposition comes up to drain the lake. One of these days, the waterbirds may be forced to flee this refuge.

When Nils Holgersson was traveling with the wild geese, a wild duck named Jarro lived at Takern. He was a young bird who had only lived one summer, one fall, and a winter. This was his first spring. He had just returned from South Africa, and there was still ice on the lake.

One evening, when he and some other young wild ducks were racing back and forth across the lake, a hunter shot at them, and Jarro was wounded in the breast. He thought he would die, but he struggled to fly. When he could fly no farther, he sank down in front of the entrance to one of the big farms along the shores of Takern.

A young farmhand happened to notice him and picked him up. Jarro summoned his last strength to nip him on the finger, but the farmhand carried him into the cottage and showed him to the mistress of the house. She gently stroked the bird on the back and wiped away the blood that had trickled down through the neck feathers. When she saw his dark-green, shining head, his white neckband, brownish-red back, and his blue wing mirror, she marveled at his beauty.

The mistress made a little nest in a basket and placed Jarro in it. He fluttered at first; but when he realized that she did not intend to kill him, he settled down and rested. Soon he was fast asleep.

A few minutes passed, and then Jarro was awakened by a nudge. When the bird opened his eyes, he very nearly died of shock. Facing him was the predator that was more dangerous than human beings or birds of prey—a hunting dog.

Oh, how the words "Caesar is coming! Caesar is coming!" had struck terror into a little yellow-down duckling's heart last summer. When Jarro had seen the brown-and-white-spotted dog wading through the reeds, he had believed that he was looking at death itself.

Caesar nosed the duck inquisitively. "How did you get into the house?" he growled. "You belong down among the reeds."

"Do not be angry with me," Jarro said. "I have been wounded by a gunshot, and people have taken me in and put me in this basket."

"Oh, I see," Caesar said. "I suppose they intend to cure you; although, in my opinion, they would be wiser to eat you. At any rate, I will not hurt you. We are not down on Lake Takern, and I am not hunting." Caesar went over to the blazing log fire and

curled up for a nap. When his beating heart was quiet once more, Jarro fell asleep too.

When he awoke, he saw that a dish with grain and water had been set within easy reach. He was still quite ill, but he felt hungry anyway and began to eat. The mistress petted him and looked pleased. After that, Jarro fell asleep again. For several days he did nothing but eat and sleep.

One morning Jarro felt good enough to step outside the basket and totter across the floor. He had not gotten far before he fell and lay there. Caesar opened his big jaws and grabbed him. Jarro believed that the dog was going to eat him, but Caesar carried him back to the basket without harming him. The next time Jarro left the basket, he went over to the dog and lay beside him. He and Caesar became friends; and every day, for several hours, Jarro slept between Caesar's paws.

Of the mistress, Jarro had no fear at all. He rubbed his head against her hand when she came and fed him. Whenever she left the cottage he sighed with regret, and when she came back he cackled his welcome.

Jarro forgot how afraid he used to be of dogs and human beings. Now he thought they were all gentle and kind. The only one in the cottage whom he did not care to meet was Clawina, the housecat. She did him no harm, either, but he did not trust her. Then, too, she quarreled with him because he loved human beings.

"You think they protect you because they are fond of you," Clawina said. "Just wait until you are fat enough. Then they will wring your neck. I know them, I do."

Jarro did not believe Clawina. He could not imagine that his mistress would harm him, nor could he believe any such thing of her son, the little toddler who sat for hours beside his basket, babbling and chattering.

One day, when Jarro and Caesar lay before the fire, Clawina began to tease, "Jarro, what will you wild ducks do next year when Takern is drained and turned into grain fields?"

"What? What did you say, Clawina?" Jarro cried. The duck jumped up, scared through and through.

"If you understood human speech like Caesar and I do," Clawina said, "you would have known what the men who were here yesterday were saying. Takern is to be drained! Next year the lake bottom will be as dry as the floor of a house."

Jarro was so angry that he hissed, "You are mean. Human beings would never do anything so cruel! Why would they make so many birds homeless? I hope that my mistress will chop off your whiskers!"

"So you think I am lying," the cat purred. "Ask Caesar then. He was also in the house last night. Caesar never lies."

"Caesar," Jarro said, "you understand human speech much better than Clawina. Tell me that she is wrong. Think what would happen if people drained Takern and changed the lake bottom into fields. There would be no more pondweed or duck food for the grown ducks, no blackfish or worms or gnat eggs for the ducklings. The reedbanks would disappear, where now the ducklings conceal themselves until they are able to fly. Where would the ducks ever find a refuge like Takern? Caesar, say that Clawina is wrong!"

The dog, who had been wide awake, laid his long nose on his forepaws and pretended to go to sleep. Clawina looked at Caesar with a knowing smile. "I believe that Caesar does not want to answer you, Jarro. Dogs will never acknowledge that human beings can do any harm.

"I will tell you why the humans intend to drain the lake. A while ago, you ducks did indeed own the lake. That was all right with human beings then; they got some good out of you. Now, grebes and coots and other birds who are no good as food have infested the reedbanks. There is no longer any reason to maintain the lake."

"Caesar!" Jarro shouted. "Caesar, you know that there are still so many ducks left that they fly into the air like clouds. Say the humans will never make us homeless!"

Caesar made a sudden spring at Clawina, forcing her to make a hasty retreat to a high shelf. "I'll teach you to be quiet when I want to sleep," he growled. "I know there has been talk of draining Takern, but there has been talk of this many times without anything coming of it. I take no stock whatever in that draining business. You know what would happen to the game if Takern were laid waste. What do you suppose you and I would have to amuse ourselves with if there were no more birds on Takern?"

The Decoy Duck

Sunday, April seventeenth.

A couple of days later Jarro was well enough to fly all about the house. His mistress petted him, and the little boy ran out to the yard and plucked young, green blades of grass for him to eat. Jarro wished that this could be his home forever.

Early one morning the mistress placed a halter over Jarro to prevent him from using his wings, and then she turned him over

to the farmhand who had found him in the yard. The farmhand stuck him under his arm and went down to the lake with him.

The ice had melted away while Jarro's wound was healing. The old, dry fall leaves still stood along the shores and mud islands, but all the water plants had begun to take root and the green stems had already reached the surface of Takern. Nearly all the migratory birds were at home. The curlews' hooked bills peeped out from the reeds. The grebes glided about with new feather collars, and the jacksnipes were gathering straw for their nests.

The farmhand got into a scow, laid Jarro on the bottom of the boat, and began to pole out on the lake. Jarro, who had now accustomed himself to expect only good of human beings, said to Caesar, who was along, that he was happy to be out on the lake again but that he did not need to be guarded so closely; he did not intend to fly away. Caesar did not reply.

The only thing that struck Jarro as peculiar was that the farmhand had taken a gun. He could not believe that anyone on the farm would want to hurt the birds. Anyway, Caesar had told him that hunting ducks was not in season yet.

The farmhand went over to one of the little, reed-enclosed mud islands. Then he got out of the boat, piled up some old reeds, and lay down behind them. Jarro was permitted to wander around on the ground, with the halter over his wings and tethered to the boat with a long string.

Suddenly Jarro caught sight of some young ducks and drakes. He remembered them. They were a long way off, but Jarro called them to him with loud shouts. They responded, and a large flock approached. Even before they landed, Jarro began to tell them about his rescue and of the kindness of human beings.

Two shots rang out behind him and three ducks sank down into the reeds, lifeless. Caesar bounded out and captured them.

Then Jarro understood. The human beings had only saved him so that they could use him as a decoy. They had succeeded.

Three ducks had died on his account. He thought that even his friend Caesar looked contemptuously at him. When they returned to the cottage, Jarro did not dare lie down and sleep by the dog.

The next morning Jarro was again taken out on the shallows. This time, too, he saw some ducks. When they flew toward him, he cried anxiously, "Away! Away! There is a hunter behind the reed pile! I am only a decoy duck!" The birds turned and went in another direction before they were within shooting distance.

Jarro had scarcely had any time to taste a blade of grass before he had to call out his warning again. He cried out as soon as a bird drew near. He even warned the grebes although he detested them because they crowded the ducks out of their best hiding places. Thanks to Jarro's vigilance, the farmhand had to go home without firing a single shot.

In spite of this fact, Caesar looked less displeased than on the previous day. When evening came, he took Jarro in his mouth, carried him over to the fireplace, and let him sleep between his forepaws.

Nonetheless, Jarro was no longer content in the cottage. When the mistress or her little boy came to caress him, he tucked his bill under his wing and pretended to sleep.

For several days Jarro continued his warning service. He had become well-known by birds all over Takern. Then one morning while he shouted his warning, "Do not come near! I am a decoy duck," a grebe nest came floating toward the shallows where he was tied. This was not especially remarkable; it was a nest from the year before. Since grebe nests can move on the water like boats, they often drift out toward the lake. Still Jarro stared at the nest because it came so straight toward the island that it looked as though someone had steered its course over the water.

As the nest came nearer, Jarro saw a little human being—the tiniest he had ever seen—rowing the nest with a pair of sticks. This little human called to him, "Go as near the water as you can, Jarro, and be ready to fly. You shall soon be free." A few seconds later the grebe nest lay near land. The little oarsman sat huddled up among branches and straw, not moving.

Suddenly a flock of wild geese flew overhead. Jarro warned them with loud shrieks, but they continued to fly over the shallows. They were just high enough to be beyond shooting distance, yet the farmhand was tempted enough to fire a couple of shots at them. These shots were hardly fired before the little creature ran up on land, drew a knife from its sheath, and with a couple of quick strokes, cut Jarro loose. The halter fell to the ground.

"Fly away, Jarro! Fly away before the man has time to load his gun again!" cried the tomten, and he ran down to the grebe nest and poled away from the shore.

The hunter's eyes were fixed upon the geese flying above him, but Caesar dashed forward and grabbed Jarro by the neck. Jarro cried pitifully. The little tomten called, "Dog, if you are as honorable as you look, you would not force a good bird to sit here and entice others to their misfortune."

Caesar grinned viciously with his upper lip, but then he dropped Jarro. "Fly, Jarro!" Caesar commanded. "You are certainly too good to be a decoy. It wasn't for this that I wanted to keep you, but because I would be lonely in the cottage without you."

The Lowering of the Lake

Wednesday, April twentieth.

Well, Caesar and Clawina no longer had Jarro to wrangle over, and the housewife missed the duck's glad quacking every time she entered the cottage. But the one who missed Jarro most was the three-year-old, Per Ola. He was the only child, and in all his life he had never had a playmate like Jarro.

When Per Ola heard that Jarro had gone back to his friends among the reeds on Takern, he begged his mother to take him down to the lake so he could persuade Jarro to return. His mother refused, but the little one was determined to find his friend.

The day after Jarro had disappeared, Per Ola was playing in the yard as usual, but with Caesar on guard. The mistress had said, "Take care of Per Ola, Caesar!"

Caesar was preoccupied these days. He knew that the farmers had held frequent meetings about the lowering of the lake; why, they had almost settled the matter. The ducks would have to go, and Caesar would never again make a glorious chase. He was so worried that he forgot about Per Ola.

The little boy soon realized that now was the time to go down to Takern and talk with Jarro. Caesar was not watching. Per Ola opened a gate and wandered down toward the lake on the narrow path that ran along the banks. He did not mean to do

anything naughty, only to persuade Jarro to come home.

When Per Ola reached the shore, he called, "Jarro! Jarro! Jarro!" He waited and waited, but Jarro never appeared. He saw birds that resembled the duck, but they flew by without noticing him. If any one of them had been Jarro, he would have stopped to talk to his friend. Per Ola was sure of that.

"Oh!" Among all the boats tied on shore, he had spotted one that was loose. Of course he could not know that the boat was a leaky old scow. He ran over to it, scrambled in, and began to rock the boat from side to side. A grown person would not have been able to move a scow out on Takern that way; but the tide was high, and the scow slid into the water. Per Ola was soon floating on Takern and calling for his pet duck.

The cracks in the old scow grew wider and wider, and water streamed in. Per Ola did not know enough to be afraid. He sat on the little bench in front, calling, "Jarro! Jarro!"

At last Jarro caught sight of Per Ola. He had been startled to hear the name he had been given by the human beings. Per Ola! Jarro was delighted to see the little boy. Why, at least one human being loved him! The duck flew like an arrow to Per Ola and let the boy caress him.

Suddenly Jarro realized that the scow was filling up with water. He squawked and quacked, but he could not make the human child understand that he must try to get to land. Jarro flew off to get help.

When the duck returned, he had a tiny tomten on his back. If the little creature had not been able to talk and move, Per Ola would have thought it was a doll.

"Pick up the pole there, Per Ola, and try to pole the boat toward a reed island," the tomten commanded.

Per Ola obeyed, and with the tomten helping him, managed to reach a reed-encircled island.

"Climb onto the island, quickly!"

Again the little boy obeyed. The very moment that Per Ola set foot on land, the scow sank. Then the child was frightened. He would have begun to cry, but a flock of big, gray birds landing

on the island caught his attention. The little tomten took him up to them, told him their names, and interpreted what they said. Per Ola was so fascinated that he forgot about being afraid.

Meanwhile the folks on the farm had discovered that Per Ola was gone. They searched the outhouses, looked in the well, and hunted through the cellar. Then they looked for him along the main roads and byways. They went to the neighboring farm to see if he had strayed over there. Of course they searched for him down by Takern.

Not once did Caesar help the people look for the little boy. He was too absorbed in his own thoughts.

Later in the day, Per Ola's footprints were found by the boat landing. Someone noticed that the old, leaky scow was no longer on the strand. Immediately the farmer and his helpers took boats in search of the toddler. They rowed around on Takern until late in the evening. Finally they reached the conclusion that the scow had gone down and the little one had drowned.

Only Per Ola's mother continued to search. No matter what anyone else thought, she could not believe that she would never see her boy again. She looked among reeds and rushes, looked and looked on the muddy shore, without giving a thought to how deep her feet sank into the mire and how wet she had become. She was desperate. Her heart ached. She did not weep, but she wrung her hands and called for her child.

Around her she heard swans' and ducks' and curlews' shrieks. They seemed to follow her, and they moaned and wailed too. "Do they worry?" she wondered aloud. "No, they are just birds. They have no worries."

Yet, the birds did not quiet down at sunset. The throngs of birds called to each other, and the air was filled with their moans and cries. The human mother thought about the draining of Takern and wondered how the thousands of mother swans and ducks and loons would take care of their little ones when the lake was gone. "It will be very hard for them," she thought.

"Where shall they bring up their little fledglings?"

She paused to muse on this. Yes, changing a lake into fields and meadows is a worthwhile accomplishment. But let the lake be some other, not Takern. Let it be a lake that is not the home of so many birds.

Had she lost her little boy at this crucial moment so that God could open her eyes before it was too late to avert the draining of the lake? She hurried back to the house and talked to her husband. She told him about the lake and the birds, and that she believed Per Ola's disappearance was God's judgment on them both. Her husband agreed that this could very well be true.

He had reason to believe this. They already owned a large farm, but if the lake were drained for farmland, their property would be doubled in size. This was the reason they had been more eager for the draining than any of the other shore owners. The others had been more cautious about the project, uneasy because the draining might prove unsuccessful and costly.

Per Ola's father had exercised all his persuasive powers to get the shore owners to agree on the draining so that one day his son might inherit a farm twice as large as the one he had received from his own father.

Had God taken his little boy away from him the day before he was to draw up the contract to lay Takern waste? "It may be that God does not want us to interfere with His order. I will talk with the others about this tomorrow, and I think we will leave the lake the way it is." His wife nodded.

The next day, while the shore owners were talking this over, Caesar was listening. When he realized that they had decided to scrap the draining proposal, he walked up to the mistress, took her by the skirt and led her to the door.

"Caesar!" she exclaimed, trying to break loose, "what do you think you are doing?" A wonderful thought came to her, and she demanded, "Caesar, do you know where Per Ola is?"

Caesar barked and threw himself against the door. She opened it, and the dog dashed down toward Takern. She ran after him. No sooner had they reached the shore than they heard a child's cry out on the lake.

Per Ola had had the best day of his life, there in the company of the little tomten and the wild geese; but now he was hungry and had begun to cry. The darkness scared him. He wanted to go home. Oh, how glad he was when his father and mother and Caesar came for him!

THE TRAVELS OF
BOOK ONE
NILS HOLGERSSON

Chapter Twenty

Ulvåsa-Lady

The Prophecy

One night while sleeping on a mud island in Takern, the boy was startled awake by the sound of oar strokes. He had hardly opened his eyes before a sharp, dazzling light made him blink.

At first he could not figure out what was shining on the lake; but as it drew nearer, Nils saw a rowboat. High on a pole in the back of the boat was a burning torch. That was the source of the bright light. The torch's red flame was reflected in the night-dark lake, luring fish to the boat.

Two old men were in the scow. One was rowing, and the other stood on a bench in the stern, holding a short, barbed spear. The rower seemed to be a poor fisherman. He was short and weatherbeaten, and he wore a thin, threadbare coat. Nils could see that he was so used to being out in all kinds of weather that he did not mind the cold. The other man was well-fed and well-dressed; he looked like a prosperous, self-satisfied farmer.

"Now, stop!" the farmer said, when they were right in front of the place where the boy was watching. He plunged the spear into the water. When he pulled it out again, a long eel came with it.

"Look at this!" he said as he removed the eel from the spear. "It's a good catch. Now I think we have enough. Let's turn back."

His companion did not lift the oars. He just sat and looked

around him. "Ah, the lake is lovely tonight," he said. And so it was. The surface of the water was still except for the gentle ripples fanning out from the back of the boat, shimmering like a path of gold in the firelight. The sky was clear and dark blue and studded with stars. All around, the shoreline was hidden by reed islands; but Mount Omberg loomed up high and dark, even more impressive than usual. The mountain cut away a huge, three-cornered section of the vaulted heavens.

The farmer agreed, after turning his head to get the torch light out of his eyes. "Yes, Östergylln is beautiful. You know, though, the best thing about this province is not its beauty."

"Oh? Then what is best about it?" asked the oarsman.

"Why, that Östergylln has always been a respected, honored province."

"Ah, well, that is true enough."

"There is more to it than that," the farmer went on. "You see, Östergylln will always be a respected province."

The rower was surprised. "Tell me how you can be so sure of that!" he said.

"There is an old story about this province," the farmer said, "and it has been handed down from father to son in my family."

"I would like to hear it," said the rower.

"Well, now, we do not tell this story to anyone and everyone; but since you are an old friend, I will not keep it a secret from you.

"At Ulvåsa, here in Östergötland," the farmer continued (and Nils could soon tell that he was reciting something almost word for word, just the way he had heard it from others), "many, many years ago, there was a lady who had the gift of fortunetelling. She had the reputation of predicting the future as accurately as though it had already occurred. People went to her from near and far to find out what was going to happen to them.

"One day, when Ulvåsa-lady sat at her spinning wheel, spinning thread, a peasant entered her home and seated himself on a bench near the door.

"'I wonder what you are thinking about, dear lady,' said the peasant after a few minutes.

"'I am thinking about high and holy things,' the fortuneteller said.

"'Oh, then I suppose it would not be proper for me to ask you about something very important to me,' replied the peasant.

"'No doubt you only want to hear that you will reap a huge grain harvest on your field,' the fortuneteller said. 'I am accustomed to receiving communications from the Emperor about the future of his crown, even from the Pope about the future of his keys.'

"'Such things must be difficult to answer,' said the peasant. 'But then, I have heard that not a person has left here without being dissatisfied with your answer.'

"The peasant saw the Ulvåsa-lady bite her lip, and he moved closer on the bench.

"'So you have heard that about me, have you?' she said. 'Well, then, why don't you tempt fortune by asking me your question? See if my answer will satisfy you.'

"The peasant immediately stated his errand. He said he wanted to know the future of Östergötland. The province was dear to his heart, and nothing would make him happier than to know what would happen to his native province.

"'Oh! Is that all you want to know?' the fortuneteller said. 'Then I think a simple answer will make you content. Why, Östergötland will always have something to boast of that other provinces cannot.'

"'Well, that is a good answer, dear lady, but I would like to know how that prediction could possibly prove true.'

"'Why do you doubt it?' asked Ulvåsa-lady. 'Östergötland is already famous! Do you think that any other place in Sweden can boast of owning two cloisters like the ones in Alvastra and Vreta or a cathedral as handsome as the one in Linköping?'

"'That may be so,' said the peasant, 'but I am an old man, and I know that people's minds are changeable. I fear that a time will come when outsiders will not give Östergötland any glory, either for Alvastra or Vreta or for the cathedral.'

"'You may be right,' Ulvåsa-lady admitted, 'but you need not question the credibility of my prophecy on that account. I can make my prediction come true. I will build a new cloister on Vadstena, and that will become the most celebrated in the North. People of high and low stations in life will make pilgrimages there, and all of them shall sing the praises of the province because it has such a holy place within its borders.'

"'I am glad to know that,' the peasant said. 'But of course, everything is perishable. What would give distinction to Östergötland if Vadstena Cloister happened to fall into disrepute?'

"'Disrepute, you say? You are not easy to satisfy; I can see that,' said Ulvåsa-lady. 'Well, I can see far enough into the future. Before Vadstena Cloister loses its splendor, a castle will be

erected nearby, and that castle will be the most magnificent of its period. Kings and dukes will be hosted there. Why, the whole province will be honored for its prestigious castle!'

"'Well, yes, I am glad to hear that,' the peasant said, 'but I cannot help thinking that this world's glories soon pass away. If the castle goes to ruin, perhaps there will be nothing at all to attract people's attention to Östergötland.'

"Ulvåsa-lady replied, 'There will be life and movement in the forests around Finspång. I can see cabins, smithies, and a great foundry. The province of Östergötland will be known for fine ironwork.'

"The peasant could not deny that he was delighted to hear this. 'Yet,' he said, 'Finspång's iron foundry might lose its prominence. If that happened, I doubt that anything else could make Östergötland famous.'

"'Ah, far in the future there will be great manors, as large as castles, built by men who have carried on wars in foreign lands. I believe those manors will also bring the province honor.'

"The peasant was not satisfied, even with all of that information. 'A time may come when people are not impressed by the large manors.'

"'Health springs will bubble on Medevi meadows, by Vätter's shores. The health springs will draw many people to Östergötland.'

"'I believe you,' the peasant said, 'but a time may come when people will go to other health springs instead.'

"'People will dig and labor, from Motala to Mem. They will build a canal right through the country, and then Östergötland will again be on people's lips.'

"The peasant still looked dissatisfied.

"'I see that the rapids in Motala Stream will begin to draw wheels,' Ulvåsa lady said. Two bright spots came to her cheeks. She was beginning to lose her patience. 'I hear hammers pounding in Motala and looms clattering in Norrköping.'

"'Even so...'

"'Oh! You say everything is perishable. One thing will remain the same: until the end of time, Östergötland will be the home of arrogant and pigheaded peasants just like you!'

"The peasant was satisfied. 'Thank you for a good answer, dear lady. You have made me very happy.'

"'I think I understand your point of view,' the fortuneteller answered.

"'The way I see it,' the peasant explained, 'everything that kings and priests and noblemen and merchants build and accomplish can only endure for a few years. But when you tell me that there shall always be peasants who are honor-loving and persevering, then I know that Östergötland will always be able to keep its ancient glory. Only those who labor forever with the soil can hold this land in good repute.'"

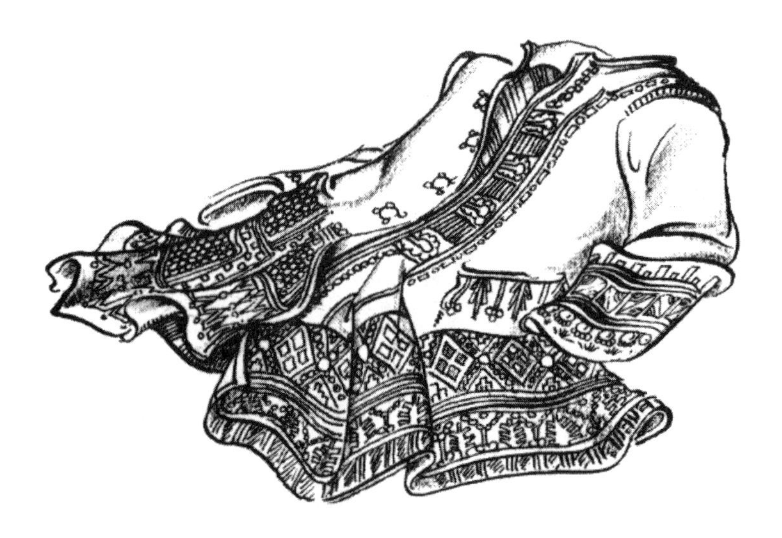

THE TRAVELS OF
BOOK ONE
NILS HOLGERSSON

Chapter Twenty-one

The Homespun Cloth

Saturday, April twenty-third.

The boy rode high up in the air, with the great Östergötland plain under him. He counted the white churches towering above the small, leafy groves around them. It wasn't long before he had counted fifty. After that he lost count.

Nearly all of the farms had large and imposing, white-washed, two-story houses. "There must not be any peasants here; anyway, I don't see any peasant farms."

The wild geese heard him, and they answered, "Here the peasants live like gentlemen. Here they live like gentlemen."

Ice and snow had disappeared on the plains, and people were out working.

"What are those crablike things creeping over the fields?" Nils Thumbietot questioned.

"Plows and oxen. Plows and oxen," his friends replied.

The oxen moved so slowly down the fields that Nils could scarcely see that they were in motion, and the geese shouted to them: "You won't get there before next year! You won't get there before next year!"

If slow-moving, the oxen were not slow-witted. They bellowed back: "We do more good in an hour than you do in a whole lifetime!"

In a few places the plows were drawn by horses. They went along with more eagerness and haste than the oxen, but the geese teased: "Aren't you ashamed to be doing ox-duty?"

"Aren't you ashamed to be doing lazy man's duty?" the horses neighed in return.

While horses and oxen were at work in the fields, the stable ram stamped around the barnyard. He was newly clipped and touchy, so he knocked down some small boys, chased the shepherd dog into his kennel, and then strutted about as though he were lord of the whole place.

"Rammie, Rammie, what have you done with your wool?" the wild geese called.

"I sent it to Drag's Woolen Mills in Norrköping," replied the ram with a long, drawn-old bleat.

"Rammie, Rammie, what have you done with your horns?"

But the ram had never had any horns, and the geese could not have offended him more than by asking why he did not have any. He was furious! He butted at the air, but of course he could not reach the geese.

On a country road came a man driving little Skåne pigs ahead of him. They were not more than a few weeks old and were going to be sold. They trotted along bravely, as little as they were, and kept close together—as if they sought protection. "Nuff, nuff, nuff, we had to leave our father and mother too soon. Nuff, nuff, nuff, what will happen to us?" they squealed.

The wild geese did not have the heart to tease the poor little creatures. As the geese flew over, they encouraged them, "It will be better for you than you could ever believe."

The wild geese were never merrier than when they flew over a flat country. Then they did not hurry, but flew from farm to farm, joking with the tame animals.

As the boy rode over the plain, he happened to think of a legend that he had heard a long time ago. He could not remember it exactly, but it was something about a petticoat, half of which was made of gold-woven velvet and half of gray homespun cloth. The one who owned the petticoat decorated the homespun cloth with so many pearls and precious stones that it looked richer and more gorgeous than the gold cloth.

He remembered this old story about cloth when he was looking down on Östergötland. The province was made up of a large plain, which lay wedged between two mountainous tracts of forest—one to the north, the other to the south. The two forest heights lie there, a lovely blue glistening in the morning light, as if they were decked with golden veils; they might have been the gold-woven cloth in the story. The plain, which simply spread out one winter-barren field after another, could have been the gray homespun cloth.

But the people on the plain must have been contented because the land was generous and kind. They decorated it with cities and farms, churches and factories, castles and railway stations. Roofs shone like trinkets in the morning light, and window-panes glittered like jewels. Yellow country roads, glossy railroad tracks and blue canals ran through the districts like embroidered loops. Linköping lay around its cathedral like a pearl setting around a precious gem. The country gardens were like little brooches and buttons.

The geese had left Öberg district and were traveling east along Göta Canal. Workmen laid canal banks and tarred the huge lock gates. In the city, masons and painters stood on scaffoldings and beautified the exteriors of houses while maids cleaned the windows. Down at the harbor, sailboats and steamers were being washed and readied for service.

The wild geese left the plain at Norköping and flew up toward Kolmården. They followed an old, hilly country

road, which wound around cliffs and ran under wild mountain walls. Suddenly the boy let out a cry. He had been swinging his legs back and forth, and one of his wooden shoes had slipped off.

"Goosey-Gander! I dropped my shoe!"

The white gander turned around and sank toward the ground. Then Nils saw that two children, who were walking along the road, had picked up his shoe.

"Goosey-Gander! Goosey-Gander! Fly up again! It's too late. I can never get my shoe back again."

Had the children seen him on Morton Goosey-Gander? He certainly hoped they hadn't.

Osa the goose-girl, and her brother, little Mats, stood looking at the tiny wooden shoe that had fallen from the sky. The girl said thoughtfully, "Do you remember, little Mats, that when we went past Övid Cloister, we heard that some farm folks had seen an elf dressed in leather breeches and wooden shoes? And do you remember that when we got to Vittskövle, a girl told us that she had seen a Goa-Nisse with wooden shoes, who flew away on the back of a goose? And then, little Mats, when we came home to our cabin, we saw a goblin who was dressed the same way; why, he even straddled the back of a goose and flew away! Maybe he was the same one who dropped his shoe from the air.

"Yes, Osa, it must have been," her little brother agreed.

The children turned the shoe about and examined it carefully, for it isn't every day that one happens across a tomten's wooden shoe on the road.

"Little Mats! Something is written on one side of it."

"I see! But the letters are almost too small to read."

"I can read them! It says…it says: 'Nils Holgersson from W. Vemminghög.' That's the strangest, most wonderful thing I have ever heard!" said little Mats.

Map of Nils' Adventures

S·W·E·D·E·N
ATLANTIC OCEAN
Arctic Cir
LAPPLAND
VÄSTERBOTTEN
JÄMTLAND
ANGERMAN LAND
MEDELPAD
HÄRJEDAL
Abisko
Luossavaara
Kiruna
Malmberg
Gällivare
Haparanda
Luleå
Piteå
Skellefteå
Umeå
Örnsköldvik
Hernösand
Sundsvall
Östersund
Sollefteå
Ljungan
L. Uman
Hornavan
BOTHNIA
OF

Söderhamn
DALARNA
Gäfle
ÅLAND IS.
Leksand
Falun
Daläls
UPPLAND
Uppsala
OSLO
WESTMAN LAND
VÄRMLAND
Mälar
Karlstad
STOCKHOLM
Örebro
SÖRMLAND
GULF OF FIN
LAKE VÄNERN
BOHUSLÄN
WEST GOTLAND
Motala
Norrköping
Trollhättan
Vättern
ÖSTGOTLAND
Gränna
Marstrand
Göteborg
Huskvarna
Visby
SCAGERRAK
Oskarshamn
GOTLAND
NORTH SEA
KATTEGAT
Varberg
SMÅLAND
HALLAND
Växjö
Borgholm
Kalmar
Falkenberg
Laholm
ÖLAND
BALTIC SEA
SKÅNE
Ring
Hälsingborg
Landskrona
Karlskrona
Kristianstad
COPENHAGEN
Malmö
Glimminge
Marsvinsholm

The Future Starts Now

Etak, with the support of Tele Atlas, is embarking on a journey that encapsulates the nature of mapping with man's curious nature to explore and discover. A fitting allegory for our future, embraced by Tele Atlas, is the popular Swedish folklore, "The Wonderful Adventures of Nils". This legendary tale is about a boy who travels the countryside on the back of a snowy white bird learning the landscape as well as important lessons about courage, kindness, potential, pride and creativity.

Just like Nils, we must fly above the horizon line, broaden our outlook and expand into new territories with confidence in our experience and knowledge. As we go forward, we'll go with all our hearts, for progress only exists if passion is at its roots.

Tele Atlas has provided a copy of "The Wonderful Adventures of Nils" for you so that you and your family can take a magical journey with Nils over the holiday season.

We are pleased you are part of our bright future. Best wishes for the new year.

The Etak Management Team